You're Never Too Old for Fairy Tales

Shirl Knobloch

. . .

You're Never Too Old for Fairy Tales

© Shirley Knobloch, 2014

Edited by: Jennifer Sabatelli

ISBN 13: 9780988517141

Also by Shirl Knobloch:

Birdsong, Barks, and Banter: Adventures of an Animal Intuitive Reiki Master and Her Home of Misfit Companions
(Available on Amazon.com)

The Returning Ones: A Medium's Memoirs
(Available on Amazon.com)

. . .

"Some day you will be old enough to start reading fairy tales again."—C.S. Lewis

For Miles Joseph......*Mr. Mooshie*......The Guiding Star to which my heart's compass points
and
Thomas Robert...*Mr. Tumnus*.......who will guide me into Narnia again someday.

Love,
Grandma

• • •

Table of Contents

● ● ●

Prologue

I have loved fairy tales ever since I could read. For a little girl bullied each day at school, fairy tales were a place of castles and princesses and *happily ever afters*. I remember huge fairy tale books, hundreds of pages long; I thought the stories would last forever. But they didn't, and neither did childhood.

I outgrew fairy tales and married and had children. Then, the fairy tales reemerged—this time, a mother telling stories to her children or watching a classic tale in front of the television screen.

Then, the children grew, and the fairy tales drifted into reality's shadows of caring for elderly parents and forging paths of my own.

Now, my someday has come.....I am old enough for fairy tales again.

I hope my readers will find hours of escape and joy here in my pages of "happily ever after," no matter how old they may be.

Princes and Kings and Butterfly Wings

Once upon a time, in a faraway land by the sea, there dwelled a brave king and his kindly son, Prince Jon. Theirs was a vast but sad kingdom. No laughter echoed through the valleys and hills, and no music soared on the wind to the sea.

Once, their kingdom had been a place of happiness and beauty. King Percival and his lovely Queen Maeve ruled with loving hearts. All in the kingdom were blessed with joy and abundance.

All except for one. The evil witch Thornella envied all that Maeve possessed. She wished for her beauty, she wished for her love, and she wished for her handsome young son.

Thornella cast a spell on Maeve, turning her into stone. King Percival was heartbroken; he could show love for nothing or no one from that day forward. Even his little son Jon was shunned by a father fearful that loving him too much would cause Thornella to take him away as well.

Joy ceased in the kingdom, except behind hushed doors. The King banned all music and flowers from filling his lands. Tiny gardens were planted in secret behind high walls. The King kept one such garden, though he never went inside. It was here that the King placed Maeve, her beautiful statue surrounded by flowers and tiny woodland creatures. Everyone was forbidden to enter this walled sanctuary. It was a forever shrine to his beautiful Queen.

Jon was not permitted here. The high walls were locked with a sturdy gate. Unbeknownst to the King, however, Jon found a small opening where a wall had crumbled. Jon disobeyed his father's decree and crawled inside. He would spend long, quiet days in the sunshine with all the flowers and tiny animals that wandered in this peaceful garden paradise. He would gaze longingly at his mother's statue and touch her cold hands and kiss her check. He missed her so. Her memory was fading. Somehow, being in the garden kept her close; he found peace within her shadow.

Years passed, and Jon grew into a handsome prince. His father grew elderly and lonelier by the year.

Then, word spread throughout the Kingdom that evil Thornella had lost a prized possession. She kept a beautiful jeweled butterfly in an iron cage at her Tower. The butterfly was like no other. Her wings were rimmed with sparkling diamonds, and set upon them lay sapphires, amethysts, rubies, and gold.

Town folk knew the legend of this beautiful Butterfly Maiden. If captured by one of them, she must be killed. A peaceful death would turn her jeweled and gilded wings to worthless dust. If killed quickly, her wings would bring Thornella's ransom.

Word spread throughout the kingdom. The villagers went searching. Finding this little treasure would mean a life of countless riches.

Jon frantically searched the countryside. He walked and rode horseback to the sea and back, searching for her. He must find this Maiden before one of the townspeople killed her for her jewels. Day after day, he searched, looking in vain and sorrowfully watching the townspeople crafting strong nets to capture her and break her beautiful wings. Doing so would tear the life from her frail, little body.

Day after day, he returned to his mother's garden, weeping at her side. He spoke to the little creatures of the forest, telling them about the Maiden.

"We have seen her," the little sparrows whispered in his ear. "We will search the skies and tell her she is safe here in this garden with you."

"Thank you, dear friends," Jon cried. Jon watched his friends set off to the sky. He sat and waited. Hours passed.

Suddenly, he saw his friends appear from the clouds. Then, a sparkling light darted quickly behind them. "The Maiden!" Jon cried.

She was the most beautiful thing he had ever seen. Her wings rivaled all the stars in the sky, and her jewels outshone the sun. She landed on a flower petal nearby, and her exquisite wings drooped with exhaustion.

"Please do not hurt me," she softly whispered. "I have only a short time left to live and wish to enjoy the beauty of your garden. Thornella never let me see or smell or taste the flowers. Nor did she let me feel the warmth of the sun or the coolness of the rain. For years, she kept me in an iron cage within the darkness of her Tower. Let me enjoy the light for only a little while. I know my wings are beautiful in your eyes, but they are not the true beauty I possess. Take care of me. Hide me and keep me safe. Then you will be blessed with far more than the sum of my jewels."

Jon cared for her. Early mornings, he would gently lift her to the most beautiful, fragrant blossoms in his father's sanctuary. Then he would place her in his mother's stone hands at night to sleep. No one dared to enter the King's garden; she slept contentedly and safely for many nights to come.

Several days on, Jon entered the garden in the early hours after dawn to find the Maiden lying on her side.

"My time in the beautiful light of your garden is ending. Now, Jon, I will share my beautiful light with you."

The tiny butterfly let out a long and heavy sigh and closed her wings tightly. The lustrous jewels turned into shriveled brown wings, just as Thornella had foretold. But Jon didn't care. He gently picked them up as if they were diamonds and cradled them in his hands.

"My beautiful friend," he cried, "how I will miss you. My garden will now be a lonely place."

Just then, a magnificent light encircled the Maiden's still body. It spread wider and wider and blanketed the whole garden in a cover of twinkling starlight. Jon's eyes were blinded by the intensity, and he held his head down. A familiar voice called to him.

"Jon, look up."

Jon looked up at his mother's statue. Only now, the stone had been turned back to flesh. Thornella's spell was broken. The Queen stretched out her arms and cradled her son in her warm hands. Her strands of hair glistened like gold, her crown gleamed with amethysts, her eyes sparkled like sapphires, her mouth was tinted the color of rubies, and her gown shone like diamonds in the sun.

Love and laughter echoed through the garden, the village, and the castle walls. Music played, and the King and Queen danced.

And somewhere in a faraway place, in a room dark as night, Thornella wept. Her tears, cold as icicles, streamed down her face. And slowly, she turned to stone.

The Mouse and the Bee

A tiny mouse and buzzing bee

A most unlikely pair

Set stow away one wintry day

On ship and paid no fare

The masts were high

The decks were dark

What shall become of us

Said buzzing bee

To tiny mouse

We should have chosen

The bus

I shall search for crusts of bread

And chew the rigging thin

For you to knit

Me warm red mittens

To place my mouse feet in

But what of me

Said buzzing bee

With water everywhere

Where shall I find

A pretty rose

Her wings abuzz with fear

Fear not, my love

Each night I'll bring

One precious rose to thee

For you have filled

My mouse-sized heart

With sail, and song, and glee

And so it was

Each night

On deck

A table vase stood bare

For one brave mouse

Who brought a rose

Back to his

Lover's lair

Beneath the decks

In a cozy nest

Filled with honey,

Bread, and love

Sailed a mouse and a bee

On adventures high

With the salty breeze above.

O Sole Meow

Pietro was an orange and white striped tabby who lived above the alleyways of Venice, Italy. He could look out the small basement window of his home and gaze out at the Doge's Palace. Though not nearly as grand, Pietro's home was comfy and warm, thanks to his loving mama.

Pietro liked the night; daytime was too busy. Hundreds of merchants, traders, and shoppers always underfoot, shooing and shouting at him to get out of the way. He usually slept until late in the afternoon and set out on his prowl as the rose-colored hue of dusk softened the Venice streets. First stop was St. Mark's Square to chase a few lingering pigeons who straggled behind. Then, it was out with his friends until the wee hours of morning.

Pietro's mother was having a birthday in a couple of days, and he knew just the purr-fect present for her. Mama had lived in Venice her entire life, met Pietro's father along the canal, and fell in love one moonlit evening in a gondola they had stowed away on.

Pietro's father had died many years earlier when his son was barely past a kitten. This birthday, Mama seemed sadder than usual and missed Papa very much.

"I know just the surprise to cheer her up," Pietro quietly whispered to himself.

"Hey, Pietro, what did you say?" his friends meowed.

"Just thinking aloud," Pietro answered. "Mama's birthday is the day after tomorrow, and I need you guys to help me with her present. I'm going to give her a gondola ride in the moonlight, just like Papa, and sing 'Happy Birthday' like the gondoliers that sing 'O Sole Mio' along the canal."

A burst of laughter broke out among his friends. "Who do you think you are, Luciano Catarotti?" they giggled. "And besides that, do you know how dangerous it is to be caught stealing a gondola?"

Pietro's mind was made up. "Are you guys going to help me or not?"

"Are you nuts, Pietro!!! Maybe you want to lose one of your nine lives if the gondolier catches you, or maybe lose part or all of your tail as he tries to snatch you up!"

Suddenly, one of Pietro's buddies, Giacomo, meowed, "I'll help." He loved Mama. She always set an extra plate at the table when he came to visit. That was a good thing because Giacomo was always hungry.

"Great!" Pietro meowed. "We'll meet around midnight and untie the gondola. Then we'll steer it down the canal past my house, and I will serenade Mama just like Papa did. Thanks, Giacomo," purred Pietro happily.

The next day, Pietro could hardly sleep a wink he was so excited. Even the pigeons wondered where he was as they lazily lingered around the piazza. All he could do was squeeze in a quick catnap. Then, he washed and brushed his fur, something he did only to please Mama because he hated baths. Even his long, straggly tail had to look purr-fect for Mama's birthday.

He raced by shopkeeper Giuseppe's stall and grabbed a red and white striped shirt from his stand. Giuseppe ran after him, but his clumsy feet were no match for the swift paws of Pietro. Now, he would look just like the gondoliers along the canal. He hurried up to his room and hid the shirt so Mama would not see it until later that evening.

Pietro went to bed early, which surprised Mama. He didn't sleep. He just stretched out on his bed, waiting for his mother to turn out the lights. Then, he crept quietly out of his bedroom window onto the terrace. His partner in crime, Giacomo, was waiting under the street lamp.

"Hurry up," he yelled to Pietro as he scurried down the window box.

"Wait a minute, I forgot my shirt!" Pietro slid back up the windowsill and quickly grabbed his red and white striped gondolier shirt. Together, he and Giacomo tiptoed on cats' paws to the dock, untied the gondola, jumped in, and started down the canal.

"I must be crazy to be doing this!" Giacomo meowed.

"Okay, we are here!" Pietro excitedly cried. Suddenly, the night silence was broken by the sounds of sweet meowing in the moonlight. Pietro shyly started to sing 'Happy Birthday,' each note getting stronger and stronger as his courage grew.

In an instant, the window shutters sprung open, and Mama hung her head out to see what was going on. "Pietro, what are you doing?"

"I'm taking you for a ride. Climb on!"

"For Heaven's sake, I'm in my nightgown. Look at my hair!"

Just then, a twinkle of moonlight shone on Pietro's face. Mother cat had never realized just how handsome he had become and how much he looked like Papa in his red and white gondolier shirt. In that twinkling, she forgot about her nightgown and her messy hair. She was a young calico again, ready to start life's journey in a gondola like so many years before.

"Jump in, Mama! We're going to see Venice in the moonlight." With that, Pietro took hold of the paddle, steering skillfully below the bridges and maneuvering the gondola down the canals of the city. In the moonlight, for just a moment, Mama looked up and could have sworn she saw her husband guiding the vessel under the starlit sky.

Pietro carefully pulled the gondola back against the edge of the canal so Mama could step down without getting her paws or slippers wet. She kissed her son goodnight and thanked Giacomo as she ascended the stairs.

Before the first light of morning, Pietro scurried to the shopkeeper's stall and neatly folded the red and white shirt back on the stand. Giacomo stood waiting to help tie the gondola dockside before any of the gondoliers arrived for work and discovered that it was missing.

"Thanks, my friend, for helping me last night," Pietro mewed.

"Glad to be of service," Giacomo meowed. "We'd better hurry. It's almost daybreak."

Mama had a nourishing breakfast waiting for her son when he arrived back at his home. Together, they had the best birthday she could have ever hoped for. Giacomo's big piece of birthday cake was set out on an extra plate, waiting for his visit.

Wishes

nce upon a time, in a kingdom that bordered an enchanted wood, there lived a king and queen in a magnificent palace. They had all that riches could buy, except for one thing.

Their little prince was born unlike the other boys of the village. A sickly infant, he grew into a fragile child. His legs were weak; he could not run. His thin arms were frail; he could not wrestle and joust and play sports with the other children. His weak body could not sit upon a horse. He spent his days in quiet thought, reading, drawing, and playing chess with the king.

The king dearly loved his boy. He searched kingdoms near and far for someone skilled in healing, but none could offer any cure. The little prince was entrusted into the care of a very loving nanny. They would slowly walk into the village on special days. There, the prince could purchase new books and drawing pencils, which he dearly loved.

On one such outing, the nanny and prince came upon the village children taunting a little dog. He was a mangy looking thing, covered in dirt and fleas, with a leg that drooped behind as he walked. The prince was weak in body, but his heart was strong and kind. He scooped up the little dog in his arms, though he used all of his strength to carry him. He bundled him under his coat and took him back to his room at the palace.

The nanny loved this child as her own; she did not tell the king. If a little dog brought this boy some hours of happiness, then he would stay. She looked beyond the dirt and the fleas and saw his kind, loving heart.

When darkness fell, the nanny drifted off to sleep. The prince stroked and brushed the little dog's fur and shared the evening meal he had not eaten with him.

At once, the little dog spoke. "I am from the enchanted woods. Because you have been so kind to me, I will grant you one wish. What is it that you desire, dear prince?"

The prince looked at the tiny dog's misshapen legs, his matted fur, and his clouded eyes. "I wish to take away your pain, dear friend. I know how it feels to be taunted by those who run and play. I wish you strong legs to run and play in the woods again."

The boy looked upon the dog's face. He seemed to be smiling.

"You have a kind heart, dear prince. You shall be rewarded."

In a moment, a beautiful angel entered the prince's room. She led him to a beautiful golden throne, which sat beside the most magnificent throne he had ever seen. "Now you shall sit beside the king of the most beautiful kingdom in the universe," the angel whispered.

When the nanny awoke, the prince was still upon his bed. By his side lay the most beautiful dog she had ever seen. His fur was the color of gold, his legs were strong and straight, and his eyes were brilliant as the sun. Upon the boy's pillow lay one large, white feather.

Fearing what the king would believe if she told him this story, she hid the dog and feather in a quiet part of the palace and then summoned the king and queen.

There was a royal funeral. No expense was spared to bid farewell to the little prince.

The nanny was given a lovely cottage at the end of the enchanted woods. There she lived the rest of her days with a loyal, beautiful dog by her side.

The feather she had placed inside the little prince's favorite drawing book. One day, the king and queen would find it...perhaps it would bring wishes of its own to them.

Brave Arthur

ne harsh winter brought hunger to the village of Briarwood.

The King issued food rations to all the town folk. The surrounding woods brought starvation to the animals, as well. There just wasn't enough greenery and seeds to soothe aching bellies.

Arthur was a brave little mouse. He often crept into the village to watch the castle tournaments. He imagined himself a brave knight. Knights helped those in distress. Arthur decided it was his noble calling to help his friends.

Arthur's strength was ebbing. He had only a tiny cache of seeds and berries nestled in his home. Yet, if a friend came calling, Arthur would gladly share. For that is who Arthur was, a brave and just knight—only one with whiskers and a long tail.

Arthur filled his backpack with four grains of wheat and a berry cake for his quest. He crept by moonlight, closer and closer to the King's storehouse. All night he worked, chewing through the wooden board until a tiny opening permitted him entrance. All his labors made him hungry. In no time, his backpack had been emptied.

Arthur was not greedy. He took just enough seeds from the storehouse to fill his backpack and went home to share the news with all his friends. Now, they would have enough grain to survive the winter.

On the way, a hungry sparrow stopped him. "Arthur, my children are starving. May I share a seed from you?"

"Yes," Arthur squeaked. "But you must promise to help me this evening."

"I promise," sparrow replied.

"Meet me at the willow tree in the glen tonight when the moon is high in sky." Arthur shared his seed with sparrow and journeyed on.

Soon, he came upon a chipmunk.

"Arthur, my tummy is growling. Please share your seeds with me."

Arthur replied, "First, you must make me a promise. Meet me by the willow tree in the glen tonight when the moon is full. I need your help."

"I promise," said the chipmunk as he scurried off with his seed.

Arthur journeyed on. Soon, he came to an opossum in the wood.

"Dear Arthur, can you spare some seeds for my babies?"

Arthur looked at two tiny faces peering out from their mama's pouch. "I will give you the rest of my seeds, but first you must promise to help me."

"I promise," said mama opossum.

"Meet me at the willow tree in the glen this evening when the moon is high in the sky. I need your help."

Arthur journeyed on to home. His backpack was empty, and so was his stomach. He reached home only to find his cupboard had been emptied. Arthur laid down to rest.

At nightfall, brave Arthur summoned enough strength to make it to the willow tree. His life was fading, but he had to finish his knight's quest.

At the willow, sparrow, chipmunk, and opossum waited. Arthur told them of the opening in the storehouse he had chewed.

"Hurry, while the moon is high. The King's guards will be watching the grain."

Arthur's friends saw how weak their friend had become. They knew his time was short without nourishment. Sparrow set off to the sky, carrying a tiny purse in her beak. Chipmunk dashed through the barren branches. Opossum ambled after.

Sparrow landed first. She filled her purse with as many seeds as it could hold and took flight back to Arthur. Chipmunk, his cheeks filled to bursting, followed after. Opossum, who left her babies home sleeping, filled her empty pouch to the brim. Arthur was at the willow, his eyes closed.

"Oh no, we are too late!" cried sparrow. She dropped her purse and chirped a soft, mournful song for her friend.

Arthur's whiskers twitched. He was alive!

Chipmunk and opossum were now at the willow as well. Sparrow carefully fed Arthur as if he were one of her baby birds. They sat with him all night until his strength was restored enough to journey home.

Then, they invited all their friends to share their feast. Arthur was made Knight of Briarwood for his bravery. His royal crest was that of a willow tree, with a full moon overhead.

That winter, he went on many quests back to the storehouse to help feed his friends. From then on, he was known as Sir Arthur of the Willow, Knight of Briarwood.

Little Heather

nce upon a time, in the land of Seven Lochs, stood the kingdom of the McConnell clan. Their lands were vast, abundant in strong, towering trees and protected by the strong thorns and willowy wisps of thistles. Sean was the greenhouse caretaker for the King. It was the season of spring, when fair maidens danced around the village Maypole.

Little Heather was a tiny seedling in Sean's greenhouse. She tried to see the villagers hustle and bustle as they hurried by, peeking her eyes above the edge of the potter's clay pot.

Heather was very smushed between the larger blooms, but she did not mind. To be honest, she was afraid of this place. All night, she imagined monsters and dragons in the shadows of the towering trees and bushes. They all cast eerie shadows on the greenhouse walls. Some even looked like the monster everyone feared in the Loch.

Every morning, Heather awoke to a sprinkling of water from Sean's watering pail. She liked to hide behind the bigger blooms to shelter her tiny, violet buds. The bigger flowers were so busy bragging about their beauty and how the Queen would surely choose one of them for the May Festival that they barely noticed little Heather. All they did was complain. They complained about how tiny the greenhouse was, with no room to spread their roots, and how they only belonged on the grand castle grounds.

Little Heather loved one thing about the caretaker's greenhouse—Mother Wisteria. Mother Wisteria was indeed a mother to little Heather, wrapping her soft leaves around her at night when she was frightened. She would cover her branches over her pot when Sean wielded his sharp garden hoe among the plants. She would catch the water from Sean's pail as it fell and let it softly trickle down her leaves so that little Heather could quench her thirst. How Heather loved Mother Wisteria!

"One day, little Heather, you must leave this greenhouse and go to a beautiful place like Heaven," Mother Wisteria whispered.

"No! I want to stay here with you," little Heather cried. But she knew that what Mother Wisteria was saying was the truth.

Many days, strange merchants would come into the greenhouse, pick up the bigger blooms, and carry them down the lanes past the taller trees. Little Heather knew she would not see them again and was scared of the day a merchant would grasp hold of the potter's clay that held her.

"Please, Mother Wisteria, promise me that I can stay and never leave you."

Mother Wisteria would wrap her branches around little Heather and comfort the small flower as best she could. "Do not worry, little Heather. You are beautiful, and one day, you will have a loving home much nicer than the greenhouse caretaker's cottage. In the morning, the comforting light of the sun will awaken you and warm your tiny shoulders. No icy water will hurt you from the caretaker's pail; only the gentle rain will caress your leaves. The soft dew of morning will quench your thirst. My mother told me of such a garden, but it is too late for me. Once, long ago, I had the most beautiful blossoms in the greenhouse. Their fragrance was the envy of all the other flowers. But now I am old. My trunk is twisted and gnarled, and my leaves are scrawny. I have grown too tired to bloom. No one will love me anymore."

"That's not true! I love you, Mother Wisteria! If I were a wealthy merchant, I would buy you and bring you to the King's garden. I promise. Please bloom for me," little Heather pleaded.

At that moment, Heather felt a gentle sprinkle of water on her leaves. It was not morning, and caretaker Sean was not passing by with his water pail. She heard a soft sobbing sound coming from Mother Wisteria. "What's wrong, Mother? Please do not cry."

"I am crying because I love you so, little Heather," she whispered. "How I will miss you when you go."

"I will take you with me," little Heather answered. Mother Wisteria smiled; she knew it would not be.

"How I wish I could go, but I am too old and too big. My home is here at the caretaker's greenhouse for as long as they will have me. One day, I will heat the castle fireplace. My place is here, little one. You must go and seek your place, my little child."

Days passed, and little Heather grew stronger, taller, and more beautiful with each one. The caretaker's water pail did not sting so much anymore; her stem had grown into a tall, straight stalk. At the top of her head were the most fragrant and beautiful purple blossoms. Little Heather knew her days at the greenhouse were growing shorter. Soon, a merchant would come and choose her pot to grasp.

This morning, Mother Wisteria gently called out to her friend. "I have a surprise for you," Mother Wisteria whispered. Wearily opening her sleepy buds, little Heather looked up and saw hundreds of tiny, violet blossoms on Mother Wisteria's branches.

"Now you *are* the most beautiful plant in the greenhouse!" Heather cried.

"It is because of you, my child," Mother Wisteria replied. "You have given me a reason to bloom again."

Later that morning, Sean was unusually excited. He went up and down the lanes, straightening each potter's clay.

"The Queen is coming!" Heather heard him announce to the merchants.

Little Heather stretched her head to see a beautiful woman, in the most elegant gown she had ever seen, walk down the greenhouse lane. She stood right in front of Heather's clay pot. "How pretty you are! You will look beautiful in my royal garden." With that, the Queen's handmaiden lifted Heather up and whisked her past all the tall trees.

"Wait!" little Heather shouted. "Mother Wisteria, I do not want to leave you! I want to see all of your beautiful blossoms open. I do not want another home, not even the royal garden. I just want to stay here with you."

"You must go, little Heather. Go and be a strong flower, and remember that I will always love you, my daughter."

Mother Wisteria watched little Heather until she could no longer see from the tops of her tallest branches. Tears of fragrant sap rolled down her trunk as she looked upon her petals for the last time.

Little Heather could not see where she was going. She was covered by a blanket and bumping along in a wagon toward the royal castle. The darkness made her drowsy, and she drifted off to sleep.

When she awoke, she felt different than she had ever felt before. There was so much room for her roots to stretch out! Her head felt warm in the brightness of the afternoon sun. A gentle sprinkle caressed her blossoms. She could see the castle walls from her place in the garden.

Then, she remembered what Mother Wisteria had told her. It *was* wonderful to be in a real garden. Little Heather felt happy and sad at the same time. She knew this was her home, and it was a beautiful one, but nowhere could ever be truly home without the mother she loved.

Days passed, and little Heather flourished in the garden. There were so many new things to see and feel. She heard little creatures singing over her head. She saw big, furry creatures run by her leaves every day. Sometimes, the Queen strolled by and touched her blossoms! Her touch was almost as nice as Mother's. How she missed Mother's arms around her.

One morning, little Heather awoke to much activity in the garden. The greenhouse caretaker, Sean, and the royal gardeners were busy milling about. A couple of them had tools like the greenhouse caretaker's hoe in their hands. Little Heather was frightened. Were they coming to take her away to another strange place?

Just then, little Heather saw the Queen's handmaiden come out to the garden. "We must hurry for the Queen," she told the workers. "Ever since she saw that old, twisted thing, she has talked endlessly to convince the King to buy it for her. Oh, the expense to haul it here!"

Hush fell over the garden as the Queen made her entrance. "I am so happy she is coming today. I have been thinking of her since I was at the caretaker's greenhouse last week. I did not know if they could move her or not. She is just like the one from my homeland kingdom. I used to sit under her branches with my own mother and dream of finding my Prince one day. I remember her twisted, gnarled trunk and all the hundreds of beautiful blossoms that smelled so heavenly. She will be the most cherished tree in my garden!!!"

Little Heather's buds opened wide with excitement as she watched the royal gardeners lift Mother Wisteria from the cart. She looked more beautiful than little Heather could have ever imagined. Little Heather had never seen so many fully opened blossoms like the ones adorning Mother Wisteria's branches.

The gardeners dug a very deep hole in the ground next to Heather, being careful not to disturb her tender roots. "Old girl, I never expected to see you leave," she heard Sean say. "Who would have thought—the royal castle! I am glad you found such a loving home," he whispered gently into Mother Wisteria's trunk.

The Queen had ribbons strung on Mother Wisteria's branches for the Maypole festival. Never had she looked so lovely.

Mother Wisteria looked down at little Heather and wrapped her branches around her. "I love you, my daughter, and we will be together from now on, always."

Little Heather loved her home. She loved the morning sun, the evening moon, and the gentle creatures that sang above her head and found a home in Mother Wisteria's branches. She even grew to love the furry creatures that sometimes lifted their legs upon her trunk. Mother Wisteria told her they were the royal hounds.

Most of all, little Heather loved her mother's sheltering arms around her. This truly was Heaven.

The Injured Bird

nce upon a time, in a far off land, lived a widowed King and his beautiful daughter, Gwen. The years had flown quickly, and the King wished his daughter to find a husband before his time on earth was spent. He announced a competition for all the neighboring royals.

"Bring my daughter the richest treasure and win her heart. Then, she will become your bride." Word spread quickly throughout the neighboring kingdoms.

Now, Gwen wasn't too happy about this contest. But her father promised that *she* alone would decide the winner.

Princes from all across the continent came. Some brought gold coins, and some brought treasure chests filled with jewels. Some brought exotic creatures from their homelands, and others brought exotic spices, fragrant teas, and perfumes.

Gwen passed each one by. Material treasures could not woo her. Her father knew this. If the right Prince came along, Gwen would know and so would he.

Seasons passed, and Gwen's father grew weaker. Princes came and went and took their treasures home with them—without Gwen.

Then one day, a wanderer came to the palace gates. In his hands was an injured dove that could not fly. Gwen was watching from her window and wondered what had caused such commotion at the gate.

"Away with you!" the palace guards yelled. "Take that sickly creature with you. Do not bring plague upon this house."

"Wait!" screamed Gwen, running toward the gate. Her loving eyes gazed upon the frightened dove and the tender eyes of the man who held her.

Not knowing that this was the Princess, the young man spoke. "I have come to offer my treasure for the competition."

"You must be jesting," the palace guards smirked.

"Bring him to Father," answered Gwen.

The young man was brought before the King and the girl he had assumed to be only handmaiden to the Princess.

"Where is your treasure?" the King asked.

The man held forth the injured dove. "I bring you this gentle being of peace. She is in need of care to mend a broken wing, as our Kingdoms are in need of peace and repair. I am Prince William, son of King Edward."

The King recognized the resemblance in the Prince's face. He and King Edward had not spoken in decades, long before Gwen was born. He did not speak; there was no need.

He watched his daughter cradle the little dove in her arms. The treasure had been accepted, its value beyond gold or jewels.

The Prince and Princess were married, uniting two troubled kingdoms in everlasting peace.

Spiders in the
Castle

ammy Spider was weaving his large web under the eave of the great hall of the castle. He was feeling very chilly and not many bugs were flying around. Not even a castle flea was hopping about.

Sammy began to feel very lonely. This was his first year away from his home web and family. He felt the gusty wind blowing in the drafty castle, bristling the hairs straight up on his eight spider legs. Every single one of his spider eyes was tearing from the cold. He tried to curl himself up in a little ball and spin some threads around him like a blanket.

Feeling very hungry, Sammy just went to sleep. When he awoke the next morning, he found much of his web had been blown apart by the cool night breezes that whistled through the castle chamber.

His spider stomach ached, and he missed all his spider siblings and his spider mom. "I should have stayed closer to home. She would know what to do," he thought.

All at once, Sammy saw a huge shadow pass over him. He was being scooped up in a big glass jar. He was very scared. All his spider web threads were scattered over him, and he felt like he was in a tempest as the container quickly started moving.

"Where am I going?" Sammy was very frightened. Then, he felt a thump as something tapped the container very loudly, making him fall right out!

He landed on a soft, velvety leaf. "This feels nice, and it is warm. Where am I?"

Sammy was in the chamber of the King's physician, Gregory. "You will do very nicely, little fellow." Gregory knew the value of spider webs. They were known to stop bleeding and help keep wounds clean. Sammy was still very frightened, but he settled down once he saw Gregory meant him no harm. Tenderly, Gregory placed the little spider on a ceiling rafter.

Sammy soon made friends with some other spiders in Gregory's care. "We are the King's spiders, and we are proud to serve his Highness with our webs. You are welcome here," they all chimed in. "It is warm and safe. Gregory has some leeches in a jar, too. They work for the king as well."

It was warm in Gregory's small chamber; the fire kept the room much cozier than the massive great hall. Sammy hid among the rafters by day. By night, he spun the neatest of webs. He listened to men talk of magic and medicine, and his webs were used to help the King's wound when he fell from his horse.

Sammy lived a long life as the royal physician's spider. He knew his mother would be proud of him.

Rat Tail, Mouse, and Pumpkin

at Tail, Mouse, and Pumpkin were best friends. They were the strays of Cork Castle. No one in the village wanted them, so they became each other's family.

Mouse was tiny and frail. His first family was a group of tenant farmers on the outskirts of the village. They wanted a dog to herd and guard their sheep. Mouse couldn't guard a fly. He didn't like to go outside. He didn't like the cold. He didn't like to get his paws wet, which wasn't an easy thing to avoid in the fields of Eire. Mouse didn't even like to go outside to the bathroom—also not a good thing in a crowded, one-room farmhouse. His family would yell, "Mouse, what is this wet spot on the floor! One more time and you are leaving!" Mouse made one too many wet spots, so his family tossed him out the door.

Rat Tail was lovable but misunderstood. He was curious and fun loving, but he always managed to get into trouble. His owner had been the dungeon guard at the castle. Oftentimes, the prisoners would hear him yell, "Dog, did you do this!" Most times, Rat Tail did. Then, his owner would grab him by his fluffy tail and throw him in one of the dungeon cells. Rat Tail's fluffy tail soon became skinny and sparse. "The next time you cause trouble, it's out the door for you!" Rat Tail saw the door close behind him very soon. Villagers saw this skinny-tailed vagrant and called him Rat Tail from then on, his first real name.

Pumpkin belonged to a family once. She was round as a pumpkin when she was a baby, so that became her name. She loved to eat; nothing was better than stealing food anywhere she could find it. Her family would yell, "You big pumpkin, you are eating us out of house and home! If this doesn't stop, you are going out!" Pumpkin tried, but she just couldn't stop eating. She climbed up on the table; she stood on her tippy toes to reach the storage bin of apples; she stole loaves of warm bread cooling on the windowsill. Pumpkin's family couldn't support themselves and a bottomless-stomached dog. Soon, she was out on her own, as well.

Birds of a feather flock together—so do stray dogs. Soon, Rat Tail, Mouse and Pumpkin were scavenging the alleyways of the village together for any scraps they could find. The air was cold and damp; it was soon to be Yule. Mouse could hardly stand it. His paws were freezing on the cold, wet ground. All that the three had for shelter was a dirty, threadbare blanket Pumpkin had stolen off a cart.

It began to snow. Village candles lit the windows of cottages. Some villagers still roamed the streets; most had been out late drinking in the tavern and yelled at Rat Tail, Mouse, and Pumpkin to get out of their way. "Get out of here, you mangy looking beasts!" Mouse was so frightened that he hid in the bushes and did a little wet spot *outside.* How he wished he had listened and not done so many in the cottage before.

Pumpkin called out to him, and the three hungry friends continued on. The snow was falling so deeply now that Mouse was almost swallowed up in drifts. He held Rat Tail's tail like a rope tied to a mountain climber as they trudged wearily on. Finally, even Rat Tail had to climb onto Pumpkin's back. He was thankful it was such a broad, round back. He pulled Mouse up behind him. The three, now bonded as one furry mound, forged on.

Pumpkin's paws were sooooo very cold. She could hardly feel them, and she was becoming very sleepy. She laid down to rest. Mouse's thin, raggedly blanket was all they had as they shared a few crusts of bread left outside the baker's shop as their Yule's Eve supper.

Suddenly, a bright light appeared, and a beautiful Angel called their names. The air around them felt warm, and Pumpkin's paws defrosted.

"It is the eve of Yule," said the Angel. "I have come to grant you each your favorite wish. Tell me what each of you desires most with your heart."

"I want a warm bed where I can just sleep all day," whispered Mouse.

"I want bowls and bowls of food and plenty of snacks to munch on," a hungry Pumpkin sighed.

"I just want to be loved," cried little Rat Tail.

Before they could blink their eyes, the Angel disappeared. Pumpkin thought she was dreaming or hallucinating from hunger, but Rat Tail and Mouse said they had seen her, too. Just then, a group of villagers singing carols of Yule walked down the path.

"What have we here," said a kind-faced woman, holding the hands of two little children. The children let out squeals of delight and scooped up Mouse and Rat Tail in their arms. Pumpkin was too big, but the boy wrapped his arms around her very tightly. "What are you doing out in the cold on this Yule Eve night?" the mother asked.

The little family took Mouse, Rat Tail, and Pumpkin home. They had a wonderful Yule feast. Pumpkin was so full she thought she might burst. Mouse found a snuggly bed to wriggle under the covers in when the little girl went to bed. He was so happy he even decided to go outside to the bathroom before bed! Rat Tail searched the house for a dungeon cell. It was all he had known—surely every cottage had one. He found none! For the first time in his life, he didn't have to be imprisoned anymore.

Days passed, and spring came. Mouse, Rat Tail, and Pumpkin stayed with their family and lived out their lives in love and safety, celebrating many, many more Yules together.

And Rat Tail's tail grew fluffy and long.

Eire

In a land where stones have faces

And spirits live in trees

And heather fills the valleys

To dance amidst the breeze

It's here that fairies wander

And magick fills the air

In a sea-kissed island yonder

In the County of Kildaire.

If you think you know what green is

If you think you've felt the rain

Well let me tell you something

That's a mystery to explain

Till you've walked the fields

Of Ireland

What you thought you knew

Was true

Can't compare to Eire's beauty

Once she casts her spell

On you.

There's a green more green

Than springtime

There's a rainbow every day

There is mischief in the woodlands

From the fairies and the fey

Yes, until you've walked

Through Ireland

Words alone cannot describe

The fair beauty of this Emerald Land

Of ancient Celtic tribes

I have seen the Fairy faces

I have heard the music reels

I have felt a peace in Ireland

A mere mortal seldom feels.

If you ever go to Ireland

In the County of Kildaire

Give the fairy folk my greetings

On this Island oh so fair.

The Music of Love

Patrick was an old man with a wrinkled face and calloused hands. He had worked hard all his life and found true love, but he lost his heart and connection to life and the living when she crossed. He lived as a hermit in the woods, passing each season with just enough to get by.

He closed his heart to friends, to love, to companionship. His only company was a tin whistle. Patrick poured his heart into every lilting note in the night. The music drifted from his tiny cottage into the surrounding woods.

Patrick did not know it, but the fairies loved him. At night, under the moonlight, they danced and twirled and courted and fell in love under the stars to his songs. The wee folk came from miles around to gather in the heather near Patrick's home. Each night, he played to an audience he never knew was listening.

The fairies always made sure Patrick never went hungry. They planted berry seeds around his cottage to give him sweet fruit. They brought the bees to give him honey. They spun tiny woolen blankets to stuff into the cottage cracks to keep the cold winds out.

Patrick played for many years. Then, one summer evening, the music was still.

The fairies crept up to his cottage and peeked in the doorway crack to see him lying silent on the cottage floor.

One brave fairy squeezed inside to touch the hand of her friend, something fairies almost never do. But Patrick was a trusted friend, a friend who never saw the face of so many who had danced and laughed and loved to his music in the night.

Patrick had left to join his own true love and dance his own jigs in another place of laughter and happiness. What should the fairies do? With all their strength, they could not lift Patrick or make a proper burial grave for their friend. So, it was decided at the fairy council to build around him. Fairies from miles around came to help. They covered his cottage slowly and lovingly in a mound of soil.

If you see a fairy mound, do not disturb it. It is a place of much respect and honor. Perhaps it is the place where Patrick rests, his tin whistle at his side, silent but never forgotten.

In the early morning, some fairy tears remain as dew in the flowers that grow on top, mourning the loss of a treasured human friend.

Friends in the Sky

olly loved to wander in the woodlands. She grew up in a small cottage near the edge of the wood. Her mother and grandma were travelers; they knew all the ancient healing ways. People would come to them for herbs and poultices. Her ma and grandma were wise in the old ways—which herbs and mushrooms to pick, which blossoms and bark could be boiled into healing teas, and where to find the fairy folk and dryads in the woods.

Molly felt safe in the woods, away from people who sometimes called her ma and grandma nasty names. To some town folk, they were the witches of the wood.

Molly possessed magick, but she was kind and filled with light, not darkness. If any little creature in the woods needed help, Molly would not hesitate to carry it home. And all the creatures in need found her; she possessed a communication with all of them. Molly's ma and grandma said her great grandma had possessed such gifts, and now Molly was the keeper of the same.

One day, a group of village men came knocking on ma's door. "Two small boys are missing. Have you seen them?" they gruffly asked.

"No," ma quickly answered and started to close the door. One of the men reached out and put his arm out to stop it. "If we find out you witches had anything to do with this..." Ma slammed the door, barely missing his fingers.

"Molly, I don't want you wandering in the woods today. And not tomorrow or the next day until I tell you it is safe."

Molly's heart sank. Her world was in the woods. The plants, the trees, and the animals were her friends. Molly spoke to all of them.

Grandma went into town the following morning. Watchful eyes told her the boys had yet to be found.

Ma was busy in the fields, and Molly quietly stole away. "Just for a little while," she thought.

A group of hawks circled above her in the sky, following her steps. They seemed to want Molly to follow, and she stepped further and further into the woods. She noticed the path had been trampled upon, as if previous feet had passed this way.

Then, she came to an old, abandoned well. Quiet cries for help could be heard from its walls. "Please help us! We cannot climb out, and Jimmy has hurt his leg and it won't stop bleeding."

There was only a fraying old rope and pail beside the well, not sturdy enough to have the boys climb. Molly searched the woods nearby for just the herbs she had seen ma and grandma use for bleeding. She tied the herbs in a bundle to the pail and rope and lowered them gently down.

"Place these on Jimmy's leg. I will go for help."

Molly started on her way back. The hawks flew ahead to guide her way. On the way, she met the search party of villagers.

"Look at that witch. See how the hawks follow beside her! She is enchanted!" They started to toss stones at her and the hawks.

"Please listen! I have found your boys. They need help! The hawks have helped me to find them. Do not hurt me or them! Come quickly, Jimmy is hurt."

The men followed and listened to the boys tell their story. They learned how Molly helped save them.

From that day forward, Molly, her ma, and her grandma were spoken of as healers, not witches, by all in the village. No hawk was ever hunted or harmed by any of the villagers from that day forward.

Dryads

The trees hold
Such magick
Wise spirits
In their Bark
Keepers of the forest
Protectors from the Dark

Oak, Blackthorn, Birch
Reaching Upward
Toward the Sky
Ivy tendrils trailing
Mistletoe
Hanging high

Magick in the forest
The Druid story tells
As the blackthorn
Keeps the knowledge
Of ancient chalice wells

Harm no ancient dryad
Hurt no wizened tree
For spirits linger
Inside
Where human eyes
Don't see......

No Webs for Emily

What are we going to do with Emily, dear?" Mama Spider asked her husband, worriedly. "I've enrolled her in all the Royal Court's best sewing classes, but she just will not listen to her teachers. Emily hasn't been eating very well lately either."

Father Spider shook his head and called his daughter down to the breakfast table. "Emily, where is your homework assignment? Have you finished your embroidery sampler yet? And how is your web coming along?"

"No, Father, I have finished neither. I don't want to make any webs. I'm not catching any flies—they're my friends! Besides, I want to be a vegetarian."

"A vegetarian??!!" Emily's father crossed each of his eight spider eyes. Mama Spider almost fainted and fell out of her web.

"Yes, Father, I want to grow my own vegetables, not eat my friends. I don't want to spend all day cooped up in the Royal sewing room. I want to help the Royal Gardner grow fruits and vegetables."

"This is all your fault, Martha," Father Spider yelled to his wife. "Why, if the Royal Court gets wind of this, I will be the laughing stock of the castle. No, not just the castle, the entire kingdom!!!"

Martha was vigorously fanning herself with her dishtowel.

"She takes after the crazy side of your family," Father added.

"My family?" Martha asked. "What about your Uncle Louie who thinks the earth revolves around the sun!!!!!"

"Stop arguing," Emily pleaded. "I am not crazy. I am just an individual. Girls can make decisions you know—it's the 14th century after all. My sewing teacher says I have quite a unique artistic ability."

Emily reached into her purse and pulled out a lovely blanket. "I knitted this myself," she proudly proclaimed.

"Good grief," Father Spider mumbled. "She knits blankets instead of webs. What are you going to do, Emily, snuggle the flies to death? Laughing stock, I tell you, laughing stock."

"Stop it, Father," Mama Spider gasped. "It's very lovely, Emily. Now, eat your breakfast, dear. I made special spiced beetle porridge."

"Yuck!!!!! None for me!" said Emily.

"You have to eat something," said Mama Spider.

Emily pulled out a tiny flask from her purse. "Lucy Ladybug gave me some dandelion soup. It is quite delicious. Want some?"

Father Spider rolled all eight of his spider eyes toward the back of his head. "That's it, young lady! No daughter of mine is taking hand-outs from a ladybug. We are spiders of the Royal Court; we have our pride and reputation to think about. This is my home, and as long as you sleep in my web, you will do as I say!"

Emily Spider kissed Mama goodbye, stuck her spider tongue out behind Father's back, packed up her knitting yarns and purse, and set off down the lane to sewing class. She was crying so hard all the other bugs asked what was the matter. All of her spider eyes were red and swollen. Gregory Grasshopper offered her a piece of his carrot candy to make her feel better. Janie Junebug said her blanket was the most beautiful she had ever seen.

"Don't worry, Emily. You can live with us at our houses," they buzzed. Emily didn't think their parents would welcome a spider into their homes, but she accepted their offers hesitantly. The little bugs convinced their parents that Emily would not eat them, and so she was taken in as a houseguest.

Each evening, after a delicious dinner of grass tea, dandelion soup, carrot candy, and whatever fruits and nuts could be found on the walk home from their castle studies, Emily and her friends sat down for a quiet evening by the fire. Emily knitted stockings for all of them, which is no easy task for a bunch of multiple-legged bug friends. She also knitted matching scarves to keep them warm on the way to their classes. At night, thanks to Emily, they all had cozy blankets in which to snuggle in their beds.

Sometimes, Uncle Louie came over to visit. He brought his telescope and let all the bugs have a view of the moon and stars. She knitted him an especially warm sweater with eight tiny armholes because night stargazing can be very chilly.

And yes, sometimes Emily packed a delicious picnic basket of apples, grapes, cheese, and bread and visited her mother for the afternoon. Father Spider stayed in his web on those days, refusing to come out. Emily would sneak him pieces of carrot candy when her mother was not watching, which was hard to do because Mama's eight spider eyes don't miss much. Mama would pretend not to notice as Father Spider tried to stuff the big pieces of candy in his mouth.

Word spread throughout the castle about Emily's beautiful knitting skills. Soon, the Queen was requisitioning silk stockings and handkerchiefs. Emily was appointed Royal Knitter for the Court. She had her own special chambers, and Lucy Ladybug and Janie Junebug were her maids in waiting. The Royal Chef prepared sumptuous vegetarian meals for all of them, using special plants Emily helped the Royal Gardner grow.

Father and Mama Spider beamed with pride; Emily was the apple of each of their sixteen spider eyes.

Of the Sea

er lived with her parents by the Irish Sea in a small village of fishermen. Her name was Meredith, Mer for short. Her father told her it meant "of the sea."

Fishermen in the village told many stories of mermaids and sea monsters and, most of all, selkies. Selkies were legendary creatures—seals who could discard their pelts and become human. Their beauty could tempt mortal men to fall in love with them. According to legend, if a selkie lost her seal suit, she would be trapped in mortal form on shore. Men would therefore hide these pelts and marry selkie women. Trapped by marriage and childbearing, these selkie women would long for but never be able to live in the sea again.

Mer loved the sea. She was permitted to play by the shore—but not too close, for an angry sea might swallow a little girl and carry her away forever. She collected seashells, sea glass, and pieces of driftwood, creating beautiful sculptures in her room. She was a quiet child, without friends. Her mood was as brooding as the sea; she always had a longing she could not understand.

One late afternoon, Mer was collecting sea glass. The sea was especially rough on this day. She spotted a young boy on the rocks, further out than he should be. Mer called to him to come back to shore.

He turned and showed a face of exquisite beauty. Mer had never seen such soulful eyes, such flowing hair. He walked over and told her his name was Connor. There was something familiar about him, though Mer was certain she had never seen him before. His was not a face one would forget.

"I am searching for something to give my sister," he said.

"Sea glass, driftwood—there are lots of pretty things washed on shore," Mer replied.

"No, something even more precious," Connor replied.

It was getting late. Mer should have begun her walk home by now. She said goodbye to this mysterious stranger and set out for home. Mer did not mention Connor to her parents for fear that they would stop her from going back the next day.

And back she went the next day, and the next, and the next after that. Each day, she found him, sitting on the rocks, gazing at the sea.

There were caves along the beach and mazes of hiding places for a treasure to be found. Mer and Connor searched new ones each day, though he would never reveal the object of his search. Mer became less and less interested in artwork and home; she longed more and more to walk the shore with Connor.

Then, one night at dinner, she let something slip about her search with this mysterious stranger. Her parents' strange expressions puzzled Mer. They forbade her to visit the shore again. How could they do this? What wrong had she done? Mer did not understand; her parents would not speak. There was only sorrowful silence in the home that evening.

The next day, Mer went to school as usual, but she took the path by the sea on her way home. She could not leave without even a goodbye. There he was, sitting on the rocks. This time, there was something in his arms.

He climbed down, and as he got closer, Mer saw it—it was a sea pelt.

The minute she saw it, Mer knew. She saw visions in her head of dancing in the sea, being where she truly belonged. As she reached for the pelt, she heard her parents cry. They had followed her home from school.

"Mer, forgive us. We found you on the shore next to the pelt and hid it so you would remain our beautiful child, the child we had prayed for. We could not tell you, for we would lose you, and now we have."

As Mer swam out to sea with her brother, she turned and saw their sobbing faces. But she was of the sea, and to the sea she had to return.

Children of the Night

oris Moskovich lived in the Carpathian Mountains of Romania. He was a tall, thin wisp of a man who darted across the mountains herding his small flock of sheep. Long, dark hair and angular features cast an ominous look to Boris's face, but this could not be further from the truth. A kinder soul never walked these mountains.

Boris had no friends, but he loved a young Romanian gypsy girl named Dracine. The two would meet in secret on quiet mountain paths after the sun had set for the day.

Certain pairings can come to no good end; such was the romance of Boris and Dracine.

One moonlit evening, what started as a gentle lover's kiss ended with a bite to Boris's neck.

"What have you done to me!" Boris cried.

"I am a child of the night, and now you shall become one, too, and walk the dark with me for eternity."

Boris was a gentle man; his heart was kind and compassionate. He would roam the hills for days looking for one lost, little sheep.

"I cannot be one of you. I will not kill! Please, Dracine, change me back or kill me."

Dracine could do neither. She loved Boris dearly. She had only wished for them to be together. Now, sorrow filled her eyes.

"I cannot undo what is done. I can only change you into something else. But that something must quench its blood thirst, just as I do. Perhaps a dog?"

"No, no!" Boris cried. He had always walked beside the strays of Romania's hills. They loved him; he could not return to them as a killer. The hand that had extended to give them food could not bring harm upon them.

"A rat perhaps?" Dracine asked.

"No, a rat might bring plague upon my country. Each bite might bring sickness and suffering death to my countrymen. No, Dracine, that I will not be."

"Then a bug, perhaps," Dracine suggested.

Boris thought for a moment. Yes, a little bug. How much harm could a tiny bite inflict from his mouth if he were a bug? Little harm to others, eternal life among his beloved Carpathians. "Yes, Dracine, I will change into a bug of the night."

With that, Dracine watched her love disappear into the night sky. Moments after, a tiny creature took flight behind him...........Boris and Dracine were together for eternity.

And that is how the mosquito came to be.

Not much effect or harm to anyone, indeed...if Boris could only have imagined.

Little Seed

other, how long will it be before I grow up?" asked Little Seed as he clung tightly to her arms. "Not that long, my child. You are strong and beautiful. One day, you will soar off on your own and land softly on a patch of earth. Then, your legs will stand tall in the warm sunlight," his mother whispered.

Many warm summer days passed. Mother and Little Seed watched merchants and King's pageants and farmers' goods cross the road. The sun shone brightly each day, and the moon rose to tell Little Seed goodnight every evening. As he grew stronger and stronger, he listened to his mother tell him to always be kind and never forget how much he was loved.

"I'll always have you to tell me you love me," Little Seed whispered.

But his mother knew better. "One day, you will find a new home, far away from me. Always remember that you are my beautiful child," she would reassure her son.

"I will, Mama," Little Seed would sleepily respond, cradled by his mother's soft, velvety leaves. "I will always have Sun and Moon to shine over me, and I will always love you."

One night, a very strong wind blew overhead. Strange, loud noises and bright lights in the sky kept Little Seed awake. Clouds covered his friend, Moon, and Little Seed sensed fear for the first time in his life. "Always remember, no matter what happens, or where you are, I love you, my child," his mother softly whispered. Little Seed was comforted and slept.

Suddenly, the winds grew stronger. His mother clutched with all her strength to wrap her leaves around him, but the storm was just too powerful. Little Seed awakened to a strange sensation. He was flying through the air, up where the moon shone!

"Mama! Mama!" he cried.

But she could not reach him. "Always remember, be kind! I love you!" she cried.

Little Seed was cold and afraid. The storm seemed endless, and the wind carried him most of the night. Finally, the night grew calm again, and Little Seed landed on a mound of grass. So exhausted was he from his journey, he fell sound asleep.

"Hey, what are you doing?" Little Seed cried, suddenly awakened by something pecking at his side. He looked up to see a strange creature with a sharp mouth, covered with something softer and fluffier than even Mama's leaves. "Who are you? What do you think you are doing?" Little Seed asked.

"I am Simon Bluejay, and I am going to eat you."

"Oh no, you are not! I have to go home to my mother. The storm carried me far away from home. Do you know the way back?"

"I do not know the way, but I can carry you a while to look," Simon answered. And with that, he scooped up Little Seed in his beak and flew off.

Little Seed peeked outside, closer and closer to the warmth of Mr. Sun. He looked down, searching everywhere for some familiar sight, but none came.

Simon grew weary. "It is time to rest," he said. "Besides, I am hungry. This is as far as I can take you."

SPLAT!!! Down on some mushy mud landed Little Seed, his body soaked through and through. But he was grateful for the ride and thanked Simon Bluejay. "I guess I have to spend another night away from mama," he thought. As he closed his tired eyes, he remembered her voice. *"I'll always love you, wherever you roam."* Comforted by his thoughts, he soon dozed off.

THUMP! THUMP! THUMP! "Hey! Can't a seed get any sleep around here?" Little Seed mumbled. Someone was pushing him back and forth in the mud. "Who are you, and what do you think you are doing?"

"I am Timothy Ant, and these are my friends, Anthony and Peter. We're taking you back to our house to store you for winter."

"You can't store me anywhere! I'm going home to my mama tomorrow. Do you know the way there?" asked Little Seed.

Timothy shook his antennae. Anthony and Peter shook their heads, too. "No," they muttered. "But we will drag you back to the forest if you like."

"Oh, thank you, that would be so kind," answered Little Seed.

THUMP! THUMP! THUMP! Little Seed had a horrible headache, but he was grateful for the ride. "Guys, can you just watch out for the rocks!"

With nighttime almost over, Little Seed decided to get just a little more rest. Suddenly, he was being scooped up by something large, fuzzy, and stinky. "Hey! Who are you, and what do you think you are doing?"

"I am Charles Chipmunk, and I am going to take you home to my nest for breakfast," he said.

"Oh no, you are not! I am going home to find my mother. Can you take me there?"

Charles said he did not know the way, but he offered to carry Little Seed part of the journey back towards the village. "Maybe your mother is there," said Charles.

"Thanks, Charles," Little Seed said. "I would be grateful for the ride."

Before he could blink, Charles had scooped him up and stuffed him in his deep cheek pouches. "Ughh! Yucky, wet chipmunk spit. This is even worse than mud!" said Little Seed. But he was grateful to be traveling again, even if the ride was wet and very stinky.

"Okay, we are here." Charles opened his mouth, and Little Seed hopped out. He looked around and could not see his mother. He did see many beautiful plants almost like his mama, but they were strange colors and shapes. Some had beautiful, long stems. Others were very small and spindly. Rainbows of colors covered their heads. Dainty ones clung close to the earth. Some had piercing thorns. Some leaves were soft and velvety like mama's, while others were spiky and hairy.

"Look what stinky Charlie dragged in!" uttered one of the spiky ones.

"Have you ever seen such a pitiful creature?" the others shrieked.

A little voice inside Little Seed's head told him this was not a very nice spot. His mama had always told him he was beautiful. She never spoke such harsh words to others. Something in his heart told him this was not the place for him.

"I am as beautiful as all of you," he cried. His words were met with only echoes of laughter from the flowers. "I may not look like any of you, but Mama told me it is not the outside that counts, but the love inside that matters." With that, the laugher grew louder.

"What's all the racket down there?" a voice squeaked. From overhead, amidst the oak's tall branches, came a bushy, dark object scampering into the flowerbeds. "Can't a squirrel catch some shut eye around here without all you flowers causing a riot?"

"Hey, Scampy, meet the new seed. Look how scrawny he is! How about some lunch? He's just enough for a quick snack," they chided.

Scampy scurried right up to Little Seed, lifted him in his squirrel hands, and shoved him in his mouth. He raced right back up the tree—luckily for Little Seed—without even swallowing.

"You will make a small but tasty tidbit for later," he said. "But now, I'll just leave you in my nest with my other stash of goodies."

Little Seed did not want to be part of Scampy's *goody stash*, so he cried out for help.

"Whoooooo's there?" came a lumbering voice from even higher up in the branches.

"It is I, Little Seed. Can you please help me?"

"I am William, Wise Owl. A storm is approaching. Just trust me, and I will get you out of here."

Just then, Little Seed heard that same crashing noise as the night he became separated from his mama. Bright lights came flashing across the sky.

"Come on," urged William. "I will carry you up to the tallest branches, too high for squirrel to climb. The wind will do the rest."

"Aren't you coming?" Little Seed asked.

"No, I wish I could, but I am so tired of hearing those gossipy, hateful flowers down there. Year after year, their voices speak always the same, that no one is good enough to join them. So year after year, they remain alone. My home is this old oak. It has been that way for many years, and I will grow old and die here. Now, you must go find your home, little friend."

Little Seed thanked William, for he indeed was a wise owl.

The other flowers shuddered in the storm, but Little Seed spread out his arms. "Mr. Storm and Mr. Wind, carry me home," he cried. With that, Little Seed was lifted high into the clouds.

Higher and higher, further along the trees, he drifted. Finally, he could not hold his arms out any longer and fell to the ground. It was dark and cold, but Little Seed was too tired to keep his eyes open.

Days passed. Little Seed was still too weary to raise his tiny head, so he buried it in the ground to rest and dream of his mother's arms. One morning, he felt the strong rays of Mr. Sun on his shoulders. He looked up to see green, velvety leaves wrapped around his head. "Mama, Mama! I found you!" he cried.

But Little Seed was alone. The leaves were his! Small, but sturdy and beautiful, just like his mother told him they would be.

"Oh, Mama!" he cried. "I wish you could see how beautiful I have become."

From deep inside his heart, he sensed her voice say, "I know, my child, I know."

Little Seed heard footsteps coming in his direction. "What kind of flower is this, Mama?" a tiny child asked. He felt the gentlest caress on his forehead.

"It's a baby sunflower. See its buds about to open?" the mother replied to her inquisitive child. "Soon, it will have hundreds of seeds."

Sunflower—Little Seed loved that name! Soon, he would have hundreds of seeds, and he would tell each and every one of them stories of his adventures. Most of all, he would tell them of his mama's love and kindness.

He liked this home, with the Sun to warm his days and the Moon to tell him goodnight. He would teach his own little seeds to be as kind and loving as Mama, for one day they would find their own places in the earth.

A Tale of Two Sisters

dwina and Elyssa were two calico felines who lived in a village on the moors. Though they were sisters, they came to live very different lives.

Edwina was just a few weeks old when a little girl named Mary found her wandering in the fields. Being the kind soul that she was, Mary bundled Edwina tightly in her shawl and took her home. That was many years before. Now, Mary had grown into a young lady, with social events and teas to occupy her time. Yes, Edwina still slept contently on Mary's warm bed, but she missed the little girl who carted her around everywhere she went.

Elyssa wasn't so lucky. Years of hard living had dulled her coat a bit, but she could still pass as Edwina's twin. Sometimes, during the day, when Edwina's cottage was empty of people, Elyssa crept up to the window ledge and visited her sister. "How lucky you are, Edwina, never to go hungry, never to be cold, never to be out in the English rain," she sighed. Elyssa envied her sister, often wishing that it had been *she* Mary found.

Though Edwina did live a life of safety and comfort, she longed to walk amidst the heather; she wished to feel the rain and wind against her whiskers; she wanted to walk the moors that Mary had read to her in storybooks. So, one spring morning, a deal between sisters was sealed with a purr.

Edwina and Elyssa would switch places for one month. At the end of the month, they would return to their normal lives.

Edwina packed her purse, some biscuits, and a warm shawl, and she straightened out Mary's bed covers before she left. Elyssa had no purse or bag to pack, but Edwina insisted she wash up in the basin outside before coming into the cottage—and especially into Mary's bed.

That evening, Mary and her family returned to the cottage. Her mother fixed a warm fire and baked some hearty stew. It was a rainy night. How happy Elyssa felt to be snug under Mary's quilt when darkness fell!

Edwina wasn't so lucky. Her tiny shawl was drenched within minutes, her fur soaked to her skin. She didn't know these moors; each noise and shadow frightened her to tears. Her paws were sore and swollen, her tummy just an empty space, and morning brought more rain. "Why did I long for the outside? I should never have left," she meowed mournfully.

Up ahead, Edwina saw a tiny thatched roof with smoke coming from its chimney. The prospect of food gave bravery to the frightened cat, and she crept closer and closer. Reaching the windowsill, she saw a little boy in bed, wrapped tightly in blankets. He seemed frail and thin. Edwina wondered if he had changed places with his brother, too, and had just come in from the cold as well.

Suddenly, the boy's mother entered the bedroom. She spotted Edwina on the windowsill and started to shoo her away.

"Mother, please don't. Can't she come in? Oh, how I would love to keep her."

Now, the little boy's mother was afraid of germs and dirt, and Edwina was the perfect picture of both. However, she loved her son and wanted to make him happy. "All right, but first she gets a bath."

Poor Edwina soon came to know how her sister must have felt at that basin. Yet, the lure of a warm fire overshadowed any anxiety over a little soap. Edwina complied.

Once inside, Edwina nestled next to the boy's cheek. She remembered that this was how it felt when Mary was a child. This was how it felt to be loved and needed, before friends and parties consumed one's life and heart.

Days passed. Edwina and the boy grew closer and closer. Elyssa was getting fatter and lazier with each day. Both were dreading month's end.

But a deal was a deal, and on the thirty first day of the month, Elyssa slipped outside and walked to the northern corner of the family's land. Edwina was waiting. It had taken her two days to find her way. She knew the little boy must be worried about her.

"Well, sister, how did you like indoor life?"

"I loved it," said Elyssa. "All I did was sleep and eat, then eat and sleep again. And you, Edwina? Have you felt the rain and the wind and the heather beneath your paws enough for one lifetime?"

"Yes," Edwina answered.

Elyssa frowned. She didn't want to go back outside. She didn't want to catch her own food, get soaked in the storms, and fear for her life when the farmer's dog sniffed out her hiding place.

"Sister," Edwina mewed, "a deal is a deal, but I don't wish to come back."

"What!?!" Elyssa loudly purred.

"I have found a loving little boy who spends his days in bed. He needs me, and I love him. Mary does not need me anymore; her home is a place of shelter but no love."

Elyssa couldn't believe her tiny feline ears. Was this true? She didn't have to go back outside? A tough life on the moors had made her long for security and safety, not love. So what if Mary spent little time cuddling with her; did not a warm meal and cozy fire more than make up for what lacked?

The sisters shook paws, promising to visit one another, and each went back to her new life.

Elyssa walked back to Mary's bed, climbing through the window she left open. Two days later, when Edwina reached the little thatched cottage, her heart nearly burst with happiness. One sister had shelter, one had love, but each had found contentment.

The Tattered Shawl

argaret was *plain*. No prince would be riding a white stallion any time soon to her door. She lived a quiet life, tending her small vegetable garden and sharing her land with a tired, old cow, some chickens, and one ornery goat named Byron.

One morning, while weeding the garden beans, Margaret spotted a tiny fairy sleeping on a dandelion. Now, people in those times were scared of the fairy folk; treat one badly, and all sorts of bad tidings could fall upon one's life and land. Margaret gasped aloud. The startled fairy woke.

"What is your wish, my lady fair?" questioned the little sprite.

"I am no one's lady fair. I have no prince or knight to set my laboring hands to rest."

"Is that your wish, then, my lady...to be a maiden fair?"

Wishes were too important to make any rash decisions. Margaret said she needed more time to decide.

"Come to the garden this eve when the moon is full," whispered the fairy. "Then, you must reveal your wish or lose it forever."

Margaret milked her old cow, fed Byron and her hens, and went back inside her cottage to dream of wishes and castles and princes. What should she choose? Fairy folk were tricksters. Suppose this was a trick and there was no wish to be granted?

Margaret reached into the cupboard and picked up an old-looking glass. She never looked into it anymore; no pretty face met her gaze. How wonderful to be pretty, to have long flaxen braids and rose-colored cheeks and lips moist as morning dew. Her lips were parched and cracked from the sun, her hair coarse and unkempt, her cheeks sallow from a life of drudgery.

If she were beautiful, she could leave this cottage and go to the King's Court, perhaps find a Royal husband. But then, she would need pretty dresses suited for a princess, not a farm girl. Her peasant frock was torn and tattered. How could she go to the Royal Court wearing this?

Then, Margaret thought of Bessie, her tired, old cow. What might become of her? No one would want a cow that barely gave a drop of milk. And her chickens—they were good friends. With barely enough grain, they always gave Margaret eggs. And especially Byron, her ornery goat—no one would give him a home.

Margaret thought herself a fool to worry about these beings. Now, she had the chance to be a beautiful maiden! What should she do? Margaret had a headache from all this wishful thinking and lay down to sleep.

She awoke just as night fell. The moon was rising high above the meadow. Just as she got up to go to the garden, a knock came at her door. No one ever passed this way before; Margaret had no friends. Who might this be?

At the door was a haggard old woman. Her black shawl was draped over her hunched frame. She asked Margaret if she might spare a piece of bread, a drink of water, and a place to rest her tired bones for just a while.

Margaret didn't have time; the moon was high by now. She started to shut the door on the old woman's face but soon stopped herself. She led the old woman to a chair, got some bread and a piece of cheese, and set a cup of water out for her to drink.

The woman's hands were gnarled and twisted. She raised the cup very slowly and took much time, with but a few teeth left within her mouth, chewing each bite.

Margaret was anxiously pacing the cottage floor. The moon was high. She hadn't even decided her wish. Would the fairy be waiting?

At last, the old crone slowly got up from her chair. She thanked Margaret for her kindness and left. Margaret ran to her garden. Beauty, riches, dresses, prince—what would she choose?

No matter now, the garden was empty. Margaret turned over all of the bean sprouts, pea pods, and dandelions. She ran her fingers through the carrot tops and the potato vines. But no fairy waited. Margaret had lost her chance; all was lost. Margaret went back to the cottage and cried herself to sleep.

The next morning, Margaret awoke and opened her eyes. Her bedroom was bright and clean, her bed made of polished oak, and a lovely looking glass hung on the wall. Margaret could see into it, but it was not her face looking back. She was young and beautiful, with long flaxen hair braided to her chest.

Was she dreaming? Margaret looked out her window. She saw Bessie, young and healthy, surrounded by chickens and little chicks and Byron bleating happily, a lovely lady goat at his side. Pretty dresses hung on her bedroom hook with exquisite lace collars and embroidered flowers of silk.

Margaret walked into the kitchen. Her cupboards were full. There were apples and plums and a basket of bread on her table.

Margaret ran outside. Her fields were plentiful. There were field hands working the soil and farm hands tending the barn and stables. She could hear the whinny of horses. Margaret was beside herself.

One of the farm hands walked up to her. "Good morning, fair lady. I am Henry. Thank you for hiring me. I will see to it that your garden flourishes."

Margaret looked upon the handsome face of this young man. Her heart pounded; he was handsome as a prince.

"I found this among the beans this morning," Henry added. "It looks old and tattered. I was going to use it for rags, but I thought I would ask you first if it belonged to you." With that, Henry extended his hands to give Margaret a tattered, black shawl.

"Thank you," Margaret answered. "Sometimes, things are not what they seem. This tattered black shawl is priceless now to me."

Margaret walked back inside her cottage, draped the shawl around her kitchen chair, and tied it. From then on, there it would remain to remind Margaret and her soon-to-be husband, Henry, that wishes can come true.

The Prince's Swan

In a beautiful glen, nestled next to a large lake, lay the Kingdom of Windford. The young heir, Prince Wallace, was a handsome lad who loved the land and the people of his kingdom. Every creature was treated kindly in Windford; no feather or fur was harmed by this gentle nation and its benevolent rulers.

Prince Wallace loved the lake. He would spend hours and hours gazing at the tranquil water or steering his small boat through its meandering curves.

On this lake lived a beautiful swan. The Prince called her Grace; he loved her dearly. He would bring her tasty corn cakes that the Royal Chef prepared upon his request. Baskets of freshly picked garden lettuce would be carried in his boat, for she was such a lovely creature.

The swan loved him back. She was such a magnificent being. Many male swans had tried to win her heart, but her heart longed only for the Prince. Swans give their hearts for life; they pair with only one. For her, Prince Wallace was the only one who could ever win her heart.

"But you are a swan," the other swans chided. "You can never be a *Princess*. He can never choose you to be his bride."

Day after day, the swan waited for the one she loved. And day after day, he came. He brought beautiful grasses and sat by the shore with her, telling her how beautiful she was. She gently laid her elegant neck in his arms as he caressed her.

One day, the Prince whispered in her ear. "I have found a beautiful bride, and we are to be married." The little swan's heart burst with happiness. Her dreams were coming true. All of the other swans were wrong; soon, she would become a *Princess.*

"Her name is Lydia," the Prince continued. "You will love her, too, little swan. She is as kind as she is beautiful."

The little swan's heart broke. As the Prince rowed away, she nestled her head within her feathers and cried. For days, she did not move. Her Prince did not come.

She became very weak. The other swans did not make fun anymore. Instead, they watched as a broken heart would soon claim the life of their friend. They brought her the most delicious morsels from the lake, but she refused to eat.

Each day, the little swan sat alone and wept.

The Prince and Lydia were married. He had not visited the swan for days. Then, he set forth on the lake to show his new bride the treasures of his kingdom and Grace, the dear swan that was his pride and joy. Lydia loved swans. She had brought her own swan, Pietro, to Windford.

To his dismay, the Prince was not able to find the beautiful swan on the lake. Beginning to worry, he continued to the shore where he had last seen her, many days before.

Here, his friend lay, softly breathing, each breath taking a little more of her dwindling strength.

"My dear swan, what has happened to you?" He gently scooped her in his arms and brought her back to his castle's garden pond. He had the Royal Chef prepare the finest food for her.

Each day, Pietro sat beside her, protecting her from the chilling wind. He had never seen such a beautiful swan. From the moment he saw her, his heart was won. He would gently preen her feathers and share all his food with her. He would tenderly stroke her neck with his and tell her his own heart had cried when the Princess took him from his home and family.

Soon, Grace's heart found room for Pietro. When she was well again, the Prince brought the pair back to the lake to share the rest of their lives together.

Swans mate for life. Pietro and Grace shared a lifetime of love.

A Mother's Love

he forest was very still this cold, December morning. Mossflower Squirrel crept carefully through the snow and ice, searching for any seeds or acorns to eat. She trudged a long distance this morning, almost to the edge of the woods in these early dawn hours. She liked to climb the tall pines and look out over the village to catch a glimpse of the Yule lights and decorations while people still lay sleeping.

Mossflower was sad this Christmas. The last of her family, old Grandmother Rose Squirrel, was no longer with her this year. Mossflower had always longed for children of her own, but nature had not granted her this wish. She tried to make the best of her first winter and Yule season alone.

Searching for food was very hard in the deep snow. Her fluffy squirrel tail was stiff and heavy, weighted down with ice. A bad storm had passed through the woods a few nights past, and all was enveloped in white. Mossflower had hidden away a small batch of seeds and acorns for the winter, but her supplies were dwindling. She feared they would not last for the coming sparse, winter months.

Just then, she looked down to see a ball of fluff on the ground. "This will make a very comfortable blanket for my nest," she thought. Scampering down the tree, Mossflower reached down to grasp it in her frozen paws. Suddenly, two enormous eyes looked hungrily into hers. This wasn't a ball of fluff—she was a baby owl!

"What are you doing here?" Mossflower cried. But the baby was too weak to respond. Mossflower gently lifted her up by her neck and carried her slowly back to her squirrel nest.

At last, she had her own little baby to care for. She had the heart of a mother; now she had a little baby to fill that heart. How happy she was!

The little owl slept all day long. Mossflower slept, too. The long walk home had exhausted this new mother. At the setting sun, the little owl awoke and cried to eat. Mossflower carefully mashed some cereal out of sunflower and dandelion seeds. The little owl made a terrible face.

"You have to eat something," Mossflower urged. But the little owl refused to open her mouth. Mossflower mashed some acorns and juniper berries and tried to push some into the baby's mouth. The little owl spit them out.

By now, Mossflower was so tired, but she was the best mother any little owl could hope to find. She stayed up with her baby all night, even though squirrels need their rest when the sun goes down. She kept trying to get the baby owl to eat. She even took a tiny stash of sweet honey she had hidden away and gave it to the baby. She licked her thirsty beak.

Mossflower knew this wasn't enough to keep the little owl alive. Now, her supplies were getting dangerously low. Mossflower loved this little baby; she named her Snowball. She loved her more than her own life and was willing to use up all of her food to try to save her, but she realized that she just didn't know how to take care of a baby owl. Without the proper food, she would grow weaker with each passing day.

A mother's love knows no boundaries. The wind was howling outside. Mossflower had very little strength left in her own skinny, weak body, but she carefully bundled Snowball tightly in an old sock she had found to line her nest. Clenching Snowball in her teeth, she started across the forest.

Her teeth chattered. She used all of her energy to shield Snowball from the bustling wind. Fresh snow had fallen; it was even deeper now. Little Mossflower's paws were frozen and cracked from the cold. Little blood drops revealed her path. But the love she felt kept her going. She remembered how lovingly Grandma Rose had cared for her. This baby needed her to reach the very end of the forest.

Mossflower had been taught never to venture that far into the woods alone. Many dangerous creatures lived there, including the owls. Adult owls could be a danger to little squirrels, Grandma had told her. Mossflower worried that the scent of the blood drops from her sore paws would draw other hungry predators to her path. Still, Mossflower had to try. The daylight was giving out; the tired squirrel could scarcely see a foot ahead of her.

"Whoooooooooooo goes there?" a thunderous voice echoed in the forest stillness. Trembling, half out of fear and half out of hunger and cold, Mossflower meekly answered. "I am Mossflower Squirrel," she whispered.

'Why have you come out in the night to our part of the woods? Don't you know we can eat a squirrel in one bite if we choose?"

Mossflower dropped the bundle from her cheeks and let Mama and Papa Owl gaze upon it with their sharp, nighttime vision.

"Please help her," Mossflower cried.

The startled owls' eyes grew even bigger than usual. "You came all this way in the snow to save this little baby's life?" they cried. The owls were amazed at the love this little squirrel had shown to one of their young. They quickly invited Mossflower into the shelter of their nest. "We will take care of her," they told the exhausted squirrel. "And we will feed and shelter you until this storm subsides as a show of our appreciation for your kindness."

Giving up Snowball was the hardest thing Mossflower ever had to do, except for saying goodbye to Grandmother Rose. She loved this little owl with all her heart, but she also knew in her heart she could not take care of her. With tears in her eyes, Mossflower got up at daybreak to leave.

"Wait!" Mama Owl told Mossflower. She led the little squirrel into a patch of trees. Inside one of the tallest pines was a tiny nest. In it cried three baby squirrels. "Their mother was killed in the ice storm a couple of nights ago. Papa and I have been trying to care for them, but they just don't seem to want to eat. They also like to stay awake all day long, if you can imagine that! Can you please help us, Mossflower?"

Mossflower took one look at the babies and knew this would be the best Yule of her life. She once again had a family of her own to care for and love. There was a handful of seeds and acorns in the nest that their mama had left before the accident. "This should be enough to help us all survive the following winter months," Mossflower thought to herself. Now, Mossflower and the babies would be well cared for until spring, bundled together tightly in their snug nest. Mossflower would teach them all the things Grandmother Rose had taught her through their winters, springs, summers, and autumns in the forest.

Best of all, Mama and Papa Owl asked Mossflower if she would become godmother to Snowball. They promised no harm would ever come to Mossflower's family under their protective owl eyes in this part of the forest.

Mossflower settled down to sleep amongst the babies. It was now Yule Eve. The stars twinkled through the tall pine branches like the lights of the festive village. She softly whispered, "Yule blessings, Grandmother Rose and Mother Squirrel; may you both rest in peace." Then, she drifted off to dream.

Thistle's Song

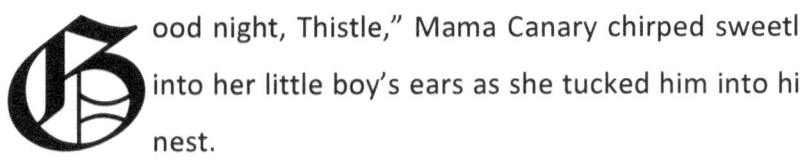ood night, Thistle," Mama Canary chirped sweetly into her little boy's ears as she tucked him into his nest.

Theirs was a gilded cage; they were the Queen's canaries. She loved them with all her heart. Each day, Thistle's father awoke the Queen with beautiful song. The Queen was delighted when Thistle's mother laid a tiny egg, more precious than any pearl in the royal jewels.

"Good night, Mama," answered Thistle. Just as Mama was pushing the little curtain to shield Thistle from the candle's light, the baby canary let out a chirp.

"Mama, I don't feel very well. My tummy hurts, and all my feathers ache. I think I will have to stay home from the royal marketplace tomorrow."

The royal marketplace was a busy affair. The Queen's royal birds would sing and welcome sellers and shoppers to the streets of the kingdom. All the royal canaries would try to sing the most intricate and lilting melody. The doves would coo, the sparrows would chirp, the crows would caw, all vying for the ears of the villagers. Thistle's father was the strongest singer in the royal flock.

Mama Canary went to put the tea kettle on. Papa Canary was sitting at the table, munching on a late snack of sunflower seed pudding. "I'm worried about Thistle, Papa. I know why he doesn't want to go to the marketplace tomorrow. It's the singing competition for all the young canaries and songbirds from neighboring villages and kingdoms."

Thistle lay in bed, staring at the shadows from the castle's candle sconces. "They're going to call me froggy again, I just know it!" Ever since he was six months old, Papa Canary had tried to teach Thistle to sing. Papa was a champion tenor; everyone in the village had expected Thistle to be the same. It had been part of Thistle's family heritage for generations. His great grandpapa had sung at the royal court, and his great, great grandpapa had sung at the King's coronation.

But when Thistle opened his beak, only frog sounds came out. Hoarse little chirps were all the little bird could muster. Mama went to the wise sage canaries for advice. She gave him soothing teas and herbs to calm his throat. Thistle practiced every afternoon, but alas, his song did not improve. Froggy soon became his nickname among the other birds. The other canaries teased him every time the royal musicians played. "Chirp along, Froggy," they teased.

One special little canary, a pretty red-headed girl, stood up for Thistle. When the other canaries started flying beside him in the castle garden, she would come very close and tell him not to listen to their taunts. The crows made up funny frog songs to caw at him. The doves cooed mournfully for his fate. The wind stung Thistle's wet eyes as he flew home to the safety of the Queen's cage.

"Tea's ready," Mama Canary said as she came into Thistle's room and gently lifted his tiny head to take a sip. "Don't worry about tomorrow, honey. The way you sound makes no difference to Papa or me. We couldn't be more proud of you and the wonderful, kind son you have become. It isn't the song that makes the canary; it is the beauty of what is inside. Your beauty, little son, outshines all the others, even those who win the competition tomorrow. Just try your best, that is all Papa and I ask of you."

"Good night, Mama. I love you," chirped Thistle. His froggy voice was music to Mama's ears. She loved him so. She wished she could shield him from the cruelty that surely faced him tomorrow.

Thistle awoke early to wash his feathers and comb them very neatly. Mama would be in the marketplace, listening to her little boy sing. Papa wished him luck.

The marketplace was very crowded with villagers. Every bird in the village waited to hear this season's competitors. Thistle looked over and saw the little red-headed girl seated on her perch.

Mama Canary flew down from the Queen's window. She looked for an empty perch and flew by several of the young birds who loved to make fun of Thistle every day. She couldn't help overhear them cackling and chirping about her little boy.

"That frog boy is going to ruin everyone's chance of winning this competition. The only reason they let him enter is because he is the Queen's canary."

Mama Canary sadly curled her beak into her feathers and slid onto a perch next to the red-headed girl. Thistle was watching and listening the whole time. He puffed up his canary feathers and rushed to his mama's side. He spread out his chest as high as he could and raised his tiny beak to yell. But no words came out. Only the most beautiful song filled the marketplace.

It was little Thistle! He had found his voice! No one could come close in the competition; he was a shoe-in for first place. His village won. Mama Canary was the proudest mother in the whole kingdom. No one would ever say cruel things about Thistle again.

The pretty, red-haired girl planted a kiss with her tiny beak on Thistle's head. His yellow cheeks blushed the same color as her rosy tinged feathers. In a few seasons, Thistle and the red-haired girl started a little nest of their own in the palace.

Thistle sang in the royal court when his papa retired to his perch. Musicians came from all the surrounding kingdoms to play beside the little bird once teased for his froggy voice.

Dandelion Dance

I wonder if the fairies

Dance

Amidst the dandelions

Such dainty seeds

So much maligned

By all of humankind

But fairies

Know these

Puffy blooms

Are friends,

Not foes,

To man

And so they dance

Among the weeds

In fairy

Flowerland.

The Heart's Wish

nce upon a time in a small village, there lived a humble fisherman and a kind-hearted baker. Each morning, the fisherman would rise before the sun, go out in his little boat, and cast his net upon the water. Each morning, the baker would rise before the sun, mix the dough for the village bread and cakes, and do her marketing for the day.

One morning, the fisherman caught a beautiful fish. His fins were golden in the early morning sunbeams. So beautiful was he, the fisherman stopped and held him for a moment before tossing him in his boat.

Much to his amazement, the fish spoke. "Spare my life, fisherman, and I will grant your heart's wish," he begged. "The spell will last one full day, until tomorrow's morning sun." He added, "Then, your wish will die, and so will you if what you've wished for has not satisfied your heart."

That same morning, the kind-hearted baker was collecting eggs in her barn as the sun rose to greet the day. She saw the most beautiful hen pecking seeds with the others. She was so beautiful, she walked over to scoop her up in her arms.

Much to her amazement, the hen spoke. "Kind woman, do not hurt me and I will grant you the wish your heart most desires. The spell will last one full day. With tomorrow's sun, if your heart has not been satisfied, the spell will die, and so shall you."

The mysteries of life and magic are hard to understand, but spells and magic often bring a price.

Now the fisherman sold his catch in the village market each day. His stall was across the way from the bakeshop. He couldn't help notice the kind-hearted baker. He loved her twinkling eyes, her brown hair always done up in a bun, and the flour-spotted apron that always covered her clothes. Sometimes, she bought fish from him. She would smile and chat and continue on with her shopping.

The baker was a kind soul. She wasn't what you would call beautiful; some might call her plain. She was the one the village men would pass by, looking at the well-dressed maidens whose hair was always perfectly in place and whose dresses weren't bleached with flour.

The fisherman was plain, his hands worn and calloused from fishing, his skin brown and wrinkled from the sun. He was too shy to speak more than a fleeting word to the baker, although his heart wished to spend the rest of his days with her.

The fisherman decided to accept the fish's offer. His wish? To be handsome as a prince and to win the baker's heart.

The baker, too, accepted the hen's offer. Her wish was to be a beautiful maiden and to win the fisherman's heart.

In an instant, both were changed. A tall, princely lad, hands soft and smooth, skin fair and untarnished by the wind and sun, stood in the boat. A beautiful maiden, long hair flowing down her back, dressed in silks and satins, stood in the barn. Both walked back to the village, hearts beating in anticipation.

The fisherman walked to the bakeshop, but his baker was nowhere to be found, only a maiden dressed in the finest clothes. Yes, she was beautiful, but she was not his love. Her silks and satins could not compare with a well-worn, flour-dusted apron and the twinkling eyes of the village girl he loved.

The baker walked to the fisherman's stall, but it was empty. A handsome gentleman looked her way. Yes, his looks were worthy of a royal position as his soft hands and fair skin proclaimed. Though he was quite beautiful, the baker only looked for the rough face and hands of a fisherman, the man she loved.

Both the fisherman and the baker went home; the sun was setting. Each listened to the beating of their broken hearts in the darkness of the night. By morning, each heart was quiet.

The baker and the fisherman were placed side by side in the churchyard. In time, a large oak grew on the fisherman's grave. Its bark was rough and strong, its leaves tarnished by the sun. A vine of ivy sprouted on the baker's grave. Its leaves were deep green, but every so often, a leaf would grow speckled with a dusting of white. As the years went by, the ivy entwined around the oak, her vines and his trunk wrapped in an embrace.

The Calico and Tabby

A calico and tabby

Aboard a ship did sail

The calico, demure and shy,

The tabby's life...

A tale

He'd wandered o'er the oceans

And sailed the seven seas

But no one stole his heart

Like the calico did seize

He brought her tempting spices

He bought her clothes of silk

He filled her saucer nightly

With stolen galley's milk

Oh Calico, say you love me

And you will now be mine

But she scoffed her nose

At Tabby

His offer she declined

He brought her Indian sapphires

And pearls from oyster shells

He brought her French perfumes

In search of wedding bells

But Calico was stubborn

She would not give her paw

For trinkets, though they sparkled

From lands the Tabby saw

"What must I give to please you?"

The Tabby meowed in vain

The answer Calico whispered

Has always been the same

"I do not want your jewels

Or finest cuts of silk.

I do not want your perfumes

I do not want your milk."

"I only want your heart,

And when it is my own,

Then we shall sail the oceans

And set our vows in stone."

"Then I will give my heart,

For I have loved you dear.

You are my precious treasure

And this my words do swear."

"We'll sail the deepest oceans.

We'll soar on winds at sea.

For you will be my sweetheart

And I, your tabby be."

The Rabbit and the Fox

Once upon a time

In a land by the sea

There lived a red fox

Who barely could see

He had a good friend

A rabbit of grey

Who helped the fox

Eat

And keep

Hunters at bay

Now why would a rabbit

Help save a fox friend?

Well it happened

One day in this kingdom

So lend

Me your ears

And I'll tell you

My tale

Of a bunny whose life

Was saved by a bale

A bale?

You might ask

Yes, a hay bale I say

The rabbit was running

From hunters that day

Then fox came along

The bunny he spied

"Come rabbit

I'll show you

A place

You can hide."

So the fox showed

The rabbit

A large bale of hay

They'd never find rabbit

So frightened this day

The hay bale was perfect

To hop in and rest

Till the hunters

Had tired

And abandoned

Their Quest

Now this rabbit and fox

Good friends they became

Till the fox went quite blind

And the rabbit quite lame

The rabbit's good eyes

And the fox's good feet

Gave safety to bunny

Who fox would not eat

For fox loved the rabbit

Two brothers they'd stay

To live in the woodlands

For the rest of their days

Fox needed the bunny

To help find his way

The bunny's slow hop

Made him quite easy prey

But fox kept his friend

As safe as could be

As safe as a hay bale

You might say to me.

The Fairy and the Sparrow

Deep in the enchanted woods, among the branches of a wise dryad tree, there lived a little sparrow and a tiny fairy. The fairy had wings of gossamer and skin the color of the pinkest rosebud.

Little Sparrow loved her and sang her beautiful songs each morning and soothing lullabies each night. Little Fairy collected the sweetest nectar from the flowers in a little bluebell cup and brought it to Sparrow to drink. The two lived together many years in the forest amidst the warmest springs and the coldest winters.

Little Sparrow was growing more fragile each winter; the snows were hard for his tiny body to endure. Fairy collected the warmest tufts from dandelions in the spring and sewed them into blankets for her friend to sleep upon in the dryad tree. They eased his fragile bones.

One day, while Sparrow was sleeping, Fairy asked the wise dryad why her tiny friend was weakening.

"It is the season of life," dryad said. "Little Sparrow has gone through many seasons, and soon, he will depart on a journey of his own."

Fairy wept tears like dewdrops on the dryad's leaves; she knew the wise tree spoke the truth. She had seen many seasons in the forest and seen many beings lie down and take a final breath of woodland air. Soon, it would be Sparrow's time. What could she do?

She thought and thought how she could thank her tiny friend for all his song and companionship through all the springs and winters of their lives. Then, an idea came to her.

The next morning, while collecting seeds for her friend in her acorn basket, Fairy visited all of the woodland birds. She flew among the trees, greeting the sparrows, the doves, the cardinals, the finches, the crows, and the starlings. She told them of her plan.

All that night, as Little Sparrow slept, the dryad tree was full of activity. Tiny treasures, bits of yarn, lace, dried flowers, ribbons, acorns and seedpods hung like tokens on wishing trees. The seagulls carried bits of sea glass to sparkle in the sunshine. Ravens carried bits of mica, glistening in the silver light of the moon, to place on the leaves. Each piece was a token of friendship and farewell to a sweet little sparrow who loved all the beings of the woods. All hung, waiting for the morning eyes of a tiny bird.

Little Sparrow lifted his weary head with the sun. All around, he saw colors and sparkles and love. In all the surrounding trees, birdsong filled the air. With all his strength, he raised his tiny head and looked upon all the beauty in the branches. Slowly, his little head lowered.

Dewdrops fell from Fairy's eyes as she watched the eyes of her dearest friend slowly close in gratitude and goodbye.

The dryad lowered his branches to softly place his friend on the earth below. Sorrowfully, each bit of lace, ribbon, flower, and glass was gently placed above his grave.

As the seasons passed, new bits of sparkle, new remnants of cloth, and new snippets of lace could always be found at the spot where a kind little sparrow slept beneath the sun, the rain, and the snow. And a pretty little fairy could sometimes be seen for a fleeting moment, her gossamer wings shimmering in the morning light.

He Wandered in a Mutt

He wandered in a mutt

One dark and dreary day

His eyes, downcast and tired

We told him he could stay

He wandered in a mutt

All knots and dirt and fleas

We had so much to teach him

To make him feel at ease

He'd never felt the hand

Of kindness on his skin

He'd never known

A pillow

He'd only known

The sin

Of cruelty

And of beatings

Of hunger and of cold

He knew only to be

The mutt

Whom man would scold

We taught him

How to sit

How to lift his paws to

Shake

The hands of those who

Loved him

And what changes it did make

He wandered in a mutt

One dark and dreary day

He stayed with us a decade

Till his final journey's way

He had so much to teach us

Of love and loyalty

Now our day is dark and dreary

Without his face to see

He wandered in a mutt

But a mutt he did not stay

For a gentleman did leave us

One dark and dreary day

The Bug Recital

Once every year in springtime, the fireflies linked their insect feet and lit up a meadow in the Kingdom of the Fairy Mound. Thousands of fireflies lit the darkness for a night of dancing and music and gaiety, where all bugs and insects and spiders were welcome.

The insect community was all *abuzz* with plans. Little bugs could not concentrate on their duties during this time. Hauling seeds for winter was overtaken by which frock to wear or which pairs of shoes to fit on eight tiny spider legs.

Distraction was a problem, especially for Miss Buzzby. Miss Buzzby owned the local dance studio. Bugs with two or more left feet lined up at Miss Buzzby's door each spring.

No one was happier than Miss Buzzby; she loved springtime. Springtime and summer were so much easier at the dance studio. Just the thought of one more afternoon untying all those sneaker laces and then zipping up all those boots left her exhausted. Did you ever stop to think of how many feet were in a classroom of little insects and spiders? Miss Buzzby has—exactly two hundred and sixty-eight. And that is not including Mildred, the centipede.

Miss Buzzby buzzed this afternoon's session to order. "It's time to make our preparations for the firefly ball. Does anyone know what their musical numbers will be?" she asked.

"I do, I do!" Mildred Centipede yelled.

"No yelling in class, Mildred. Now, just raise one of your feet"—no problem for Mildred since she had ninety-nine more to spare—"and tell the rest of the class what you will be performing."

Mildred had a ballet number memorized. She had been practicing long hours after school at Mrs. Millipede's school of gymnastics and ballet. The twin beetles, George and Ringo, were of course performing their usual rock and roll duet. Lucy Ladybug chose a jazz routine for her debut. Charlie Cricket was still undecided. Gary Grasshopper was doing a very special number this year; his Uncle Shamus had taught him an Irish jig. His mother had sewn him a special headband and fashioned heels to the bottoms of his shoes. His number was from *Riverdance*. "That sounds like quite an undertaking, Gary," buzzed Miss Buzzby. "I am sure you will look quite handsome."

"Now has everyone decided?" Miss Buzzby added.

Irma Spider raised one of her eight legs in the air. "Miss Buzzby, this year I am going to tap dance for the school." With that, Irma jumped into the air and started tapping her legs very loudly against the bark chip floor.

"Irma!" Miss Buzzby screamed, raising her buzz above all the racket Irma's legs were making. "Let's keep some of your energy saved for when we hold our first rehearsal."

"Sorry, Miss Buzzby," Irma sighed.

This year, the moth brothers, Martin and Milton, were working the sound system. They usually were the spotlight crew, being as they were so attracted to lights, but the fireflies were handling all the lights for the ball, so the moths took over audio for that night. Charlie Cricket, the usual soundman, would be the usher and seat everyone. Charlie was happy about this since he still couldn't decide on a dance routine. Audio was a challenging job with all the buzzing and chirping among the audience. Charlie was excused from performing so he could concentrate on being usher.

Three weeks until the ball. Miss Buzzby held a fifteen-minute class every afternoon in preparation. Bugs have short attention spans; fifteen minutes was the max before they fidgeted in their seats. She was delighted with the progress all the student bugs had made. Everyone was upset when Irma Spider sprained one of her ankles tapping, but Miss Buzzby put some ice on it, and Irma was back tapping in no time.

Invitations to the ball arrived. Miss Buzzby wrote out the program. Finally, the night of the gala arrived. It was a balmy evening. The fireflies had been flying in all day.

Jenny Ladybug, Lucy's mom, baked cookies in the shape of little spring flowers. Becky Grasshopper, Gary's mom, made her special carrot candy. It was nearly dusk; time to begin.

Gary Grasshopper was the first performer. He opened the show, his sequin headband sparkling in the glow of the fireflies. It was perfect until his headband slid down over his grasshopper eyes, and he bumped into one of the set decorations. Everyone pretended not to notice. Gary finished his number without any more mishaps. Miss Buzzby said he did an excellent job.

Lucy Ladybug finished her jazz solo to thunderous applause. Then came Irma Spider's number. Irma was extremely nervous; all of her legs were trembling. The dandelion soup she had for lunch was making strange noises in her spider stomach. The music began, and Irma started tapping. Suddenly, one of her tap shoes flew wildly into the air. Bang!!! It knocked Charlie Cricket right on top of his antenna.

Charlie fell to the ground. Miss Buzzby and Mrs. Grasshopper came running. Irma was mortified! She had secretly had a crush on Charlie since bug kindergarten. Now, he probably hated her. She started to run off stage, but Charlie yelled. "Wait, Irma, please finish your dance for me."

Irma tied her shoe back on and double knotted the laces this time. She began tapping her heart out, better than she had ever danced before. Everyone in the audience gave her a standing ovation. The crickets rubbed their legs together in unison, and the fireflies dimmed their lights for a second to honor her triumph. Charlie was on his feet, though his antenna was slightly drooping. Mr. and Mrs. Spider were very proud of their daughter.

Next came Mildred Centipede. Irma was a tough act to follow, but Mildred daintily rose on one hundred tippy toes to a beautiful rendition of *Swan Lake*. Mrs. Millipede beamed with pride as she watched her star pupil perform.

George and Ringo closed the recital with a very loud and raucous rendition of the jitterbug. There wasn't a foot not tapping or an antenna not swaying to the beat in the entire meadow.

When the show was over, everyone came back on stage to take their bows. Miss Buzzby was presented with a bouquet of wildflowers. Then, all the guests were invited to the refreshment table. All the bugs agreed that this was the best recital ever as they flitted about the table. Becky Grasshopper's candy was a big hit as usual. Everyone remarked how tasty Jenny Ladybug's cookies were. Miss Buzzby even asked for the recipe. Thirsty bug mouths quenched themselves on nectar and dew.

Then, the night of dancing began. Irma walked shyly up to Charlie and asked if his antenna felt better. She apologized.

"Don't worry, Irma," Charlie smiled as he continued, "it's practically all healed. I thought you were the best dancer," he chirped.   Irma's spider heart was beating almost as fast as her tapping feet when Charlie asked her to dance.

The Sparrows

In a massive stone tower

A princess would cry

Her only friends

Sparrows

Whose wings fluttered by

Oh sparrows, dear friends

Can you please set me free

To walk the green valleys

And see what you see?

The sparrows kept vigil

From high on the hill

For a time when the

Princess's

Captor lay still

While he slept

By his side

The Tower key lain

Through the window

Brave sparrows

Tucked to loosen its chain

They pecked and they pulled

Till the clasp, it did break

Off in haste to the Tower

They soared for her sake

They gave her the key

And bid her goodbye

Then the sparrows

Left crying

Tears fell from the sky

For they loved the dear princess

With her left the light

Now the Tower held darkness

And no more delight

For the poor little sparrows

Now left all alone

Their hearts broken in two

Their wings still as stone

But an Angel from Heaven

Came down from the sky

On her wings did she carry

These sparrows up high

To the highest green valleys

With blue skies above

To reward these dear sparrows

Such beings of love.

In a Gilded Cage

nce upon a time, there was a beautiful woodland. There were towering oaks, filled with birds and squirrels. Hares and badgers, groundhogs and opossums, and all manner of furred and feathered beings lived in peace.

In the valley stood a formidable castle. A mighty king and his gentle daughter lived within its fortressed walls. The king liked riches. His subjects were treated fairly but held with little regard. His regard was for jewels, coins, richly woven tapestries, and exquisitely sewn furs.

His daughter, Julia, held little regard for such. She would wear no fur crafted by the palace seamstresses. She would place no jeweled tiara upon her tiny head. Her days were spent wandering through the peaceful woodland, her favorite spot being near an aged oak. There, a tiny bird would perch and sing each day, her song more lilting than any court musician.

This little bird was not only beautiful; she was kind. The beings of the woodland all loved her. Each morning, she awoke them with the sun. Each evening, she helped their babies to sleep with a good night lullaby. All loved her, but especially Julia.

Now the king, with all his flaws, loved his daughter. There was not a treasure upon the earth that he would not acquire for her. He ordered his servant to capture the bird and bring her back to the palace. He commissioned a gilded cage to be waiting in Julia's room.

The bird was so gentle that capturing her was easy. They trapped her, carried her back to the palace, and placed her in her golden prison.

Julia was not pleased. "How could you do this, Father? Let her go!!!!" Julia tried, but the cage was locked. The king held the key.

The little bird perched quite still; she would not sing. Julia tried to feed her tiny morsels from her tray, but she would not eat. Each night, Julia lay in bed listening to very quiet, mournful peeps, her own eyes laden with tears.

Julia's heart grew heavier each day. She sat quite still; she barely ate. The king was stubborn. He would not give in. Days passed.

One morning, the little bird lay very still on the cage floor. The king was summoned. "Throw that thing on the rubbish pile!" He handed his servant the key, and the little bird was flung out the window onto the trash heap. Julia was beyond despair.

That evening, although she was weak from not eating, Julia gathered up the strength to steal away while the king was feasting at his banquet. She found the little bird, carried her to the aged oak, and placed her on the ground. "Now you are home," she whispered to her little friend.

The evening air grew quite cold. Julia was shivering. She headed home to the palace. Afraid for all his riches, the servants had locked the palace door. Julia could not get in. She lay shivering in the cold all night.

All night, the beings of the woodland were busy, as well. The spiders spun a soft shroud of finest silk for their beloved bird. The hares wove a dainty wreath of dandelion blooms for her tiny head. The groundhogs dug a soft hole, and the foxes brought moss to line it with. They buried the little friend they loved so much by the moonlight.

In the morning, Julia's servant found her room empty. The king summoned a search of the palace and the woods. Soon, she was found, sick with high fever and chills.

For days, the king sat by her side, his eyes laden with tears. No riches in the world could make her well, though he would gladly give any of them.

Julia died. The king ordered the finest golden casket. The richest embroidered silks were sewn into her shroud. The most exquisite jewels were crowned upon her head.

The King chose the towering oak to be her sacred resting place. Little did he know, a little bird already waited there.

The Loss of a Friend

Pretty statues on the floor

Pictures in their frames

Snuggly throws and pillows fringed

Candles bright with flames.

All these make a comfy home

This I've thought for sure

But none brings joy and comfort

With your furry face

No more.........

There is no store to wander

No catalog online

To bring what has been lost

Back to this heart of mine......

So, as you sit

Amongst the finer things in life

Remember what is priceless

Those riches without price.

No statue ever smiled

When I walked through the door

No picture ever barked

To see my face once more

No pillow ever held my hand

With loving little paws

Yes, I have lost my dearest friend

Who loved me, with all flaws.

I Wonder If the Leaves

Fall is approaching
I wonder if the leaves are waiting,
Waiting
Like us for Autumn
Waiting
For harvests, and hayrides, and scarecrows
Leaves wait, as well,
Knowing
They soon will fall to earth.
We wait too.
Not knowing
Which season
Will be our time of journey
Back toward earth.

But,
We must have faith
That,
Like the leaves,
The force that created our thoughts
Will let us
Live again
Like the towering oaks
That grow from tiny acorns
Falling
Back toward earth.

My Mourning Path

(Written on the anniversary of my mother's and my little dog's passing)

The earth and sky

Last night did quarrel

Thunder shouts

Lightning cast her

Glaring eyes.

Gentle rains

Did tear upon

The sodden ground.

Rains of forgiveness

The earth

The sky

Embraced.

Were it so easy

To embrace

Those Lost on this

Sad day.........

My heart

Would shine with happiness

And burn my soul's

Dark night

With each step

Strolled

Along my

Mourning path.

Stillness

The stillness of a park bench

Beneath the rustling leaves

Calls to my hurried heart

Where my weary soul

Bereaves

The rhythms of the ocean

The music of the tide

Invite my soul to linger

Along the shoreline side

The whispers of the raindrops

The ping against my pane

The quiet stroll at twilight

Amidst a shady lane

The twinkling stars at midnight

The glow that moonlight casts

These beckon inner longings

And memories of the past

The myths and fairy tales

The legends of the knights

The spirits and the woodland sprites

All stir my soul's insights

I long for times when

Maidens

And men of valor fought

I seek the ancient

Wisdom

The druid sages taught

When hurried hearts

Did linger

And heed a primal call

Entwining breaths and heartbeats

And joining one to all.

Epilogue

In a world overshadowed by technology, violence, and maturity attained far too soon, I think we all could use some fairy tales, stories of hope and "happy endings" and lessons to be learned. Negativity and sorrow are plastered before our eyes every second with each internet post and tweet, and that negativity darkens our hearts.

As the sparrows soared to their *happily ever afters* in one of my poems, I wish my stories help lift your hearts and spirits, even if just for a little while. May they teach kindness and compassion for all beings and show the true treasures in life.

I hope you share these stories with your own children and grandchildren. I wrote them with the intention of sharing them with my own two little grandsons when they are old enough to understand.

And someday, when they have grown many years past the point of understanding, I hope they return to my fairy tales and smile. For we are never too old for fairy tales.

Wishing all of you *happily ever afters,*
Shirl

You can visit my artist gallery link to view my fairy watercolor paintings at:

http://shirlknoblochwillowfineartprintsandphotography.zenfolio.com/

Love and Light,

Shirl

www.ingramcontent.com/pod-product-compliance
Lightning Source LLC
Chambersburg PA
CBHW021055130626
46552CB00005B/2108